THE MAN WHO LIKED SLOW TOMATOES

THE MAN
WHO LIKED
SLOW TOMATOES

K. C. CONSTANTINE

DAVID R. GODINE · PUBLISHER
BOSTON · LONDON

First published in the U.S. in 1982 by
David R. Godine, Publisher, Inc.
306 Dartmouth Street
Boston, Massachusetts 02116

First published in the U.K. in 1982 by
Kudos & Godine, Publisher, Ltd.
45 Blackfriars Rd.
London SE1 8NZ England

Library of Congress Cataloging in Publication Data

Constantine, K. C.
  The man who liked slow tomatoes.

  I. Title.
  PS3553.O524M3   813'.54   81-47321
  ISBN 0-87923-407-5   AACR2

British Library Cataloging in Publication Data

Constantine, K. C.
  The man who liked slow tomatoes.

  I. Title
  813'.54   [F]   PS3553.O524
  ISBN 0-906293-05-7

First edition

Printed in the United States of America

THE MAN WHO LIKED SLOW TOMATOES

The clocks on Muscotti's back bar showed the same time as Chief Mario Balzic's watch: 3:30. Had Balzic been able to flee the sour squabbling in Rocksburg's City Hall, nothing short of a natural disaster could have stopped him. The police union contract had expired a month ago, and since then the Fraternal Order of Police had been privately making ugly noises about what they were capable of doing in the event of a strike; the mayor and some city councilmen were haranguing Balzic publicly and privately to take a more "visible" role in the negotiations for a new contract, and his men were performing in a suspicious, collective snit because he wasn't taking sides publicly or privately. All Balzic knew for certain today was that if he hadn't sneaked out of the negotiations when he did he would have choked. The smoke from the cigarettes, cigars, and pipes clung to his clothes and hair; the smoke from the needs and resentments and psychological and political games was clogging his mind.

"Give me a glass of wine," he said to Vinnie, the bartender. "The Mondavi please. Not the everyday stuff."

"Oh. And hello to you too," Vinnie said.

"Just gimme the wine."

"How 'bout some tomatoes? You want some tomatoes? I got
tomatoes up to my ass."

"Is this a saloon? Or a farmers' market? You a bartender or a
huckster?" Balzic sighed, loosened his tie, and produced cur-
rency from his pocket. "The wine? Please? Look, I even have
money."

"Okay, okay," Vinnie said, walking away and returning
quickly with a new bottle of Mondavi Cabernet Sauvignon
from a beer cooler. The bottle began immediately to stream
with condensation as he worked an opener into the cork. "No
kiddin'! You really got money?"

"Hey. You really got tomatoes?" Balzic felt confident that
Vinnie didn't.

"Yeah," Vinnie said, nodding strenuously. "I'm telling ya. I
got tomatoes."

After the financial gibberish Balzic had been listening to since
early morning, this was an argument that made wonderful sense.

"What the hell're you talking about you got tomatoes. This is
June the what, what's the date today?"

"June fifteenth, that's the date."

"Hell, that's the — is this the fifteenth already? Christ. Well,
still, the only way you got tomatoes is some amateur hijacked a
truck from Florida." Balzic took a long, slow sip of the Mondavi. There were days when to serve it as cold as it was in his
glass was a sin. This wasn't one of them. It made his mouth mel-
low and his heart full. There was joy in living yet — if, after you
spent your day helping to create a new union contract, you
could drink wine like this.

Balzic swallowed the aftertaste and said, "So? Where'd you
get tomatoes? You don't own a hothouse, nobody you know
owns a hothouse, you never bought a tomato you ever sold in
your life, and it's June. Where'd you get tomatoes?"

"You got it, you got it. Everything you say is true. That's
right. But look here. What are these — grapes?" Vinnie said,
reaching under the bar and bringing up a chip basket of fully
ripened tomatoes.

"Hey," Balzic said, and felt himself gaping. "Where the hell'd you get those?"

"Jimmy Romanelli. He brought me three baskets. What d'you think of that?"

"I'll be goddamn. I never saw tomatoes in June from around here. He really grow 'em, huh?"

"Yeah. He really did. So you want some, or what?"

Balzic looked at Vinnie and took another sip of the wine, now warming slightly from the bar's heat and from his fingers. "How much?"

"Hey, you know how much I paid for tomatoes yesterday —"

"How much, how much? Forget what you paid. How much?"

"Dollar for six. The whole basket for four-fifty."

"Come on."

"Hey," Vinnie said, "you know when you get that price? At three-thirty in the morning in Pittsburgh out of the boxcars, that's when. No other time."

Balzic rubbed his lips and sipped his wine. "Gimme a dozen. You got a bag or do I got to have my own?"

Vinnie stepped back and put his hands on his hips. "Hey, Mario, you're a smart ass lately, you know that? I mean, nobody can say nothing to you. For the last couple weeks you been a pain in everybody's ass around here. You ain't the only one with troubles."

Balzic felt his face grow warm. He looked down at his hands and then he rubbed his chin for a few moments. "Uh, what can I say?" he said finally. "So, I'm, uh, giving my friends a pain. I'm sorry."

"You don't have to apologize. Everybody around here knows your guys are gonna go on strike. Everybody knows all those clowns in City Hall are on your back. I mean, everybody knows that. But what the hell do I look like — the mayor?"

Balzic shrugged apologetically. "Hey, come on, pour yourself something."

"I don't want no drink," Vinnie said. "Just a little consider-

ation for what I am. Not much. Just a little. And when you talk
to me like I'm some asshole on city council, that don't make it."

Balzic shrugged again. "It, uh, won't happen again."

"Yes, it will," Vinnie said. " 'Cause that's how you are. But
every once in a while, somebody got to tell you."

Balzic started to reply to defend himself, but the phone rang,
and Vinnie hustled away to answer it.

"Hello," Vinnie said. "Hi, honey . . . No, he's not here . . .
No, I ain't seen him since yesterday, dear, when he brought the
tomatoes . . . Now why would I make up a story about that,
honey? . . . I would never do that . . . No I would not . . .
Listen, Franny, I don't make up stories like that when people are
upset the way you are, nossir . . . All right . . . Yes I will,
dear. The second I see him . . . And you sit down and put a
little brandy in your coffee. He'll be back . . . Nothing happened to him. He'll be back, you'll see . . . He probably went
on a little toot, you know, blow his horn a little bit, he'll be okay
. . . Okay, dear, don't worry, I'll tell him to call you right away
. . . Okay. Bye."

Vinnie rolled his eyes at Balzic, stopped to fill the beer glasses
of the two patrons to Balzic's right at the bar, and came quickly
to stand before Balzic with the bottle of Mondavi in his hand.
He waited for Balzic to empty his glass and then filled it.

"What was that all about?" Balzic said.

"The guy that grew the tomatoes? That was his old lady. He
didn't come home from here yesterday."

"Who's that?"

"Romanelli, Jimmy. He used to work the mines out in Westfield Township. You probably seen him around. He ain't done
nothing since they shut down last year. He run out of unemployment checks. He can't get welfare 'cause he owns his house."
Vinnie wiped the bar. "He's all right, but he's a jagoff, you
know. Always gotta be right."

Balzic shook his head no, meaning he didn't know this Romanelli, but there was a buzz of recognition from somewhere about
something, he wasn't sure what.

"Well, if you don't know him," Vinnie said, "you know his wife. You know her father. Her mother's dead. Franny her name is. Mary Frances Fiori. Her old man's Mike. He was big in the union with your dad. Now don't tell me you don't know him for crissake!"

"Hell yes I know him. Mike Fiori, my God. Is he still alive?" Balzic said, shaking his head in pleasant disbelief. "Hell, he must be eighty."

"Yeah, he's about that, seventy-nine, eighty, Jimmy was telling me yesterday. And he's a bull. Still works his garden every day, still walks five, six miles every day, cuts his own firewood, cooks, cleans house, takes care of himself. . . . Course he had to do all that shit. He never got married."

"He never got married again?"

Vinnie shook his head. "Nossir. Hell, you didn't know that? Sure you know that."

Balzic shrugged. "Guess I forgot."

"Yessir, boy, he raised that girl himself. Christ, she was only just a little kid when his wife died. I'll bet she was two or three, maybe four years old. Hey, that was no picnic either. But he's a stubborn fucker. Never took no shit from nobody."

"He never did," Balzic said, now feeling uneasy twitches of guilt for having lost contact with the old man. "I'll be damned. I thought he was dead —"

"What're you talkin' about — did you go to his funeral?"

"Come to think of it, no —"

"What the hell is it with you? Whatta you mean 'Come to think of it no'? Your old man and Mike Fiori were tight. D'you forget that, huh? If you forgot that, you oughta be ashamed of yourself for crissake."

"I am."

"You oughta be. . . . No, hell, he's alive. He's gonna be a hundred, that guy. Jimmy was telling me yesterday, old Mike spent fifty-five years underground — imagine! Fifty-fuckin'-five years in the mines! Started when he was thirteen. And that was all pick and shovel shit too."

Balzic nodded thoughtfully, reflecting on why he'd let him-self lose touch with a man with whom his father had shared much. "Yeah, those guys were a separate breed."

Balzic thought of Mike Fiori, and of his father, and of men like them, who spent their working lives underground, hacking out bituminous coal with picks and shovels, much of the time un-able to straighten up and frequently on their knees. Balzic shuddered. He hated the mines. He never felt claustrophobic, there was never a situation he could find himself in that would give him that feeling, but all he had to do was think of a coal mine and his chest would grow tight and his breathing would start to come in huffy, little spurts. He felt an inordinate sense of guilt for not being able to control that and then he felt stupid about feeling guilty, but it happened every time. All he had to do was think of a mine and there it all was. He emptied his glass and motioned to Vinnie to fill it.

"What's the matter with you?" Vinnie said. "You get a chill?"

"Huh? No. I was thinking about something. Hey, what's this guy's name again?"

"What guy?"

"The guy with the early tomatoes."

"Oh, Romanelli."

"What's he, uh, about forty, huh?"

"Yeah. I told you that," Vinnie said.

"He's doing a little business, huh?"

"What business? His old lady works and he makes a garden."

"No, no. He's doing some business. I been hearing that name. From the state guys, state drug guys." Balzic cocked his head and peered at Vinnie over the rims of his glasses. "What's he doin'? Huh?"

Vinnie looked away disgustedly and leaned under the counter and spit into an empty beer carton he used for garbage. "Are you kiddin' me? Huh? He ain't doing nothin'. He couldn't do no business. I told you, he's a jagoff, he's always gotta be right. Gotta have all the answers. Nobody does business with anybody like that. Maybe once. Not twice. Everybody ain't as stupid as jagoffs like that think they are. So after a while, who does he do business with? He got to move. He got to find new first-time business. But he ain't movin'. He's makin' a garden."

"Maybe I got the wrong guy," Balzic said with a shrug. "But there's a Romanelli with an audience."

Vinnie put his hands on his hips and pretended to look at traffic through the front window. "Drug guys, huh? What're they looking for?"

"Hey," Balzic said, hunching over the bar, "you're a member of the organized criminal element, how come —"

"The what?" Vinnie said hotly.

"— how come you don't know what they're looking for?"

"The what am I part of? Huh? The organized what?" Vinnie's voice moved up half an octave.

"Get yourself together," Balzic said, grinning mischievously. "What do I know what they're looking for? They never tell me. Maybe it's because the only place they ever find anything is in the lockers in the high school or the community college. Marijuana I guess. That stuff everybody's making a million dollars a minute on — if you believe the newspapers — down there in Florida and Texas and wherever. Speaking of which, why don't you retire to Florida and go into the importing business?"

Vinnie looked out the window again for what seemed a minute. He grew almost pensive. Then he said very seriously, "How many guys you think are gettin' killed down there in all that sunshine 'cause they can't talk Spanish?"

Before Balzic could reply, the phone rang again. It didn't take long for Balzic to realize that the caller was the same woman who'd called earlier in search of her husband. From Vinnie's expressions and tone it was apparent that she was close to hysteria.

"Listen, Franny . . . whoa, dear . . . Franny, I can't understand you when you talk and cry at the same time . . . okay, you take a second to get some calm, thatta girl . . ." Vinnie shook his head and looked at the ceiling and scratched his throat. "I told you before, dear, I haven't seen him since he left yesterday . . . Well why don't you believe me? What am I, a rat or something that lies to you? . . . Frances, dear, nobody does the same thing day after day every day. Sometimes you got to vary the routine or, uh, you know, your brain turns to tomato paste. Everybody —"

Vinnie thrust the phone outward from his ear and winced. Then he motioned to Balzic as though to say, here, you come talk to her.

Balzic put up both hands and shook his head emphatically. "Nothing doin'," he muttered into his wine as he took another sip. He rolled it on his tongue and held it there a second before swallowing. It was bad enough that he let a friendship with Mike Fiori slip away through neglect; he wasn't going to open it up by talking to Fiori's daughter. There were memories there too: when he was a teenager and she was a child, he watched her while their fathers talked. He thought of her then as a cousin, though there were no blood ties, and thinking of those times now as he had not in many years made his neglect of her father a more pointed shame.

". . . you called the hospitals from here to where?" Vinnie's eyes bulged at the thought of how many hospitals she had called. "And the state police . . . and the Rocksburg police . . . uh-huh, and the Rocksburg cop didn't want to know nothin', huh?" Vinnie put his hand over the mouthpiece and said to Balzic in a shouted whisper, "Hey, you hear what your guys want to know, huh? This girl's worried about her husband and your guys are gettin' snotty with her. Here, you talk to her."

"Aw bullshit," Balzic said.

"Come on, come on, doctor, give this girl some word medicine, give her a prescription. She ain't listenin' to me."

Balzic pulled his glasses down the bridge of his nose and scowled at Vinnie. "You don't understand. I haven't talked to her in years and —"

"Hey, she don't want to renew acquaintances. She wants to find her old man."

Balzic got up and went down the bar toward Vinnie, who was jiggling the phone back and forth and looking decidedly relieved.

"What was all that shit before about what friends were doing to their friends, huh?" Balzic said. He took the phone and pretended to throw a punch at Vinnie who ducked away, chortling and clucking under his breath at having rid himself of a problem.

"Hello, Mrs. Romanelli, this is the chief of police. Can I help you?" Balzic had no intention of identifying himself more fully.

There came the sound of a nose being blown. Then a pause. "What're you doing there?"

"Never mind that, Mrs. Romanelli. What's the problem? Your husband stay out all night, is that it? And he never did that before?"

"It wasn't just all night. It's almost a quarter after four. He left here yesterday around two o'clock. He called me at work to tell me. I haven't seen him since yesterday morning."

"Mrs. Romanelli, uh, was he acting any different lately? I mean, I heard from Vinnie that he lost his job and he ran out of unemployment checks, so there could be, well, a lot of pressure there. Did he show anything —"

"No," she interrupted him. "Nothing like that. He was like he always was. That's why he should've been home long ago."

"Well, okay, so, uh, how was he traveling? Car, driving his own, riding with somebody, walking, how?"

"He was walking. I had the car."

"And where do you live? Does Vinnie know?"

"Yes. He knows." She was having great difficulty speaking. Her breath was coming between sobs.

"Mrs. Romanelli, how about his friends? Have you —"

"I called them all up. Nobody — nobody seen him."

"Uh-huh. Well, look, is there somebody you can be with, some friend or relative, your father maybe? Vinnie tells me he's still alive and in great shape. He was a friend of my father's. Maybe you could stay with —"

"Why?"

"Because you're, uh, you sound very upset, Mrs. Romanelli. I mean I can understand that, but it's not good to be by yourself if you're really —"

"I'm staying right here."

"Oh. Okay. Well, I'll send a man down there to talk to your neighbors and he'll probably want to talk to you. And we'll do some checking, Mrs. —"

"Some checking!" she shouted. "There's something wrong! I'm telling you! He's never done this before. Never! You better do a lot more than just some checking, I'm telling you. I can't believe this. I can't be —"

"Mrs. Romanelli, just take it easy. You're not going to do anybody any good getting worked up more than you are."

"Don't tell me that! Help me! Something's wrong! My husband . . . my husband —" She couldn't continue. Her sobs became a wail, and the phone clicked off.

Balzic hung up the phone and went back to his stool. The bar was starting to fill again. It was just minutes after four and workers on the eight-to-four shift were coming. They came in waves in the afternoon: they started at 3 P.M., ordering beer, a shot, or both. In and out in five minutes. New ones came at 3:30, and more again at 4, and again at 4:30 and 5, and, finally, at 5:30. In good times, watches were set against their comings and goings; in bad times, complaints were measured in empty stools. Balzic heard Mo Valcanas say once that if a man wanted to know how the country was doing he could learn as much by counting customers every day in Muscotti's as he could by reading the *Wall Street Journal.*

They were here now, today's 4 P.M. wave, and the cash register was binging. Balzic figured that for every bing the cash register made, Vinnie made twenty-five cents at least and that was merely habitual. When Vinnie's wife had a hunger for something, Vinnie could make half a dollar a bing and look at the world with a gaze unwavering, direct, and pure. Balzic sat fascinated.

Here he was, not five feet from where Vinnie was making change, and Balzic could not see it happening. He knew it was happening, he had known it was happening for years and had watched it for years. He was watching it yet again and though he could practically see Vinnie's two front pant pockets swell,

Balzic could not describe to his own satisfaction how Vinnie achieved his daily rake.

Balzic shook his head in admiration. The owner, Dominic Muscotti, paid Vinnie the minimum wage allowed by federal law and thus contributed the minimum in local, nuisance, and state and federal income taxes, unemployment and insurance payments, and Social Security in Vinnie's name. Vinnie, in turn, also paid the minimums. Then, through an agreement of long standing, Vinnie stole whatever he thought he deserved, the agreement consisting of a game wherein Muscotti believed he was the victim of theft and would fire Vinnie (or worse) if he should ever catch him and Vinnie believed he could steal as much as he needed to live provided he was never caught, because if he was ever caught he wouldn't deserve to be working in a place where he could steal that much.

And, if the two of them could be heard talking about it, as Balzic had heard too many times to recount, it would sound as though Muscotti and Vinnie had, by some perversity, trapped themselves in perpetual hatred of one another or else they had arrived at the perfect way to screw the government at every level out of whatever tax the government believed it deserved. As Vinnie said so often, "Hey, Dom could get screwed by Uncle Sugar or by me. And he knows me. May as well get screwed by somebody you know, right? Who wants to get it from some tax guy every three months when I can do it to him every day?"

Vinnie's argument was founded on something more durable than logic; there grew in his bones an unshakable knowledge of the systematic, organized, and foolproof ability of governments to screw the governed, which knowledge in turn inspired in him a duty to resist governments at every level by screwing them. To Vinnie it was all reduced to an emotion as close to patriotism as he could muster: America was great because where else could you cheat on your taxes the way you could in America? "You think I could get away with this kind of shit in Russia? Fuck those commies. Imagine a country where everybody's the boss, holy shit. . . ."

"How do you do it?" Balzic said finally.

"How do I do what?" Vinnie said, washing glasses.

"I been watching you for years, and I'll be goddamned if I can spot it."

"Why you fuckin' dummy. Some cop you are." Vinnie wiped his hands dry on the same rag he used to polish the bar. "You keep looking for magic. Fast hands. The hand's quicker than the eye and all that shit. I told you a hundred times. It ain't magic. It's arithmetic!" Vinnie's voice, loud under the most ordinary circumstances, grew to a roar in a crowd. He spoke in a range somewhere below a tenor's but above a baritone's and always as though he were practicing to make a speech. In somebody else this combination might have been an affect; in Vinnie it was completely natural, though there had always been a suspicion among some of Muscotti's regulars that Vinnie was a little deaf and that's why he talked so loud.

"It ain't Houdini stuff. It's all up here," Vinnie said, tapping his temple. "I'm the world's fastest adder, subtracter, multiplier, and divider."

"Lots of people can add fast."

"Yeah? Let me tell you something. If addin' fast was punches, I'd be the heavyweight champ of the world." Vinnie surveyed his bar, saw that all orders were filled, folded his bar rag, laid it down, and then picked it up again and slapped it back on the bar.

"I thought you was gonna send one of your guys down to talk to Franny."

"Huh?"

"You heard me. Ain't you gonna do that — after you told her? What kind of shit is that?"

"Oh come on, an unemployed guy doesn't come home one night and I'm supposed to send a man to investigate? There are better things to do. If she calls again maybe I will, but I got to give it twenty-four hours at least."

"She told me it was."

"No, what she said was she hadn't seen him since yesterday morning, but you saw him. He look in any danger? Was he even drunk?"

"No."

"Well, she called how many hospitals? I thought your eyes were gonna come out of your head when she said how many. And the cops. And his friends. Right? What do you think happened?"

"He probably found something," Vinnie said with a mock leer.

"Uh-huh. That's what I think too. And when he washes the lipstick off and figures out a good story, he'll go home. He have any money yesterday?"

"Sure he had money. Couple of twenties maybe. A ten. Some ones."

"You paid him for the tomatoes?"

"Sure. Yeah."

"He have anything to drink?"

"Couple of beers, that's all."

"Say where he was going?"

"No." Vinnie stared at the bar in thought. "No. He just left. About five."

"You got any reason to think something's wrong?"

Vinnie shrugged. "What the hell do I know — I don't live with him."

"Well, do you?"

"No. I guess not."

"Then don't ask why I'm not gonna send somebody to talk to her because if the neighbors don't know anything, the trail stops with you. So then what? . . . Fill it up again. I need this wine today, my friend. I need it today."

Balzic had not set foot in his living room, nor kissed his wife, nor asked about his mother or daughters. His wife held up three tiny squares of paper.

"Three calls? Since the time I left Muscotti's to here, three calls?"

His wife handed him a sandwich freshly wrapped in alumi-num foil. "This'll hold you for a little while."

Balzic bent forward to kiss his wife.

She drew back in mock horror. "Your lips are all purple. Let me see your teeth."

"Why?"

"I want to see what color they are."

"They're a different color from my lips."

She shook him playfully. "Come on, open up."

"What's gonna happen? Aren't you gonna kiss me if they're the wrong color?"

"Open up."

"What color you like?"

"Mario, open up."

"My gums are still the same color, I bet."

"Mario, if your lips are purple you had a lot. And if your teeth are purple you —"

"Had too much, I know."

"Come on, let me see."

Balzic shook his head resolutely. "I'm going back to work. And I ain't gonna let nobody see my teeth except my mother and I already know she don't care what color they are, she loves me anyway. G'bye."

He started out the door and then turned back. "Hey, Ruthie baby, are those calls urgent urgent or can I just call 'em back and find out what they want and tell 'em I'm tired and gotta lay down for a while, huh?"

"If your eyeballs weren't as purple as your lips, you'd know the answer." She canted her head and said, "Why don't you listen to me? I tell you over and over to drink white wine so they have to at least get close enough to smell you."

"Sometimes you got to have red." He turned and went out the door and was halfway down the front steps before she could react.

"Why do you sometimes just got to have red?"

Balzic never looked back. She asked him again. Balzic was concentrating too hard on not tripping down the steps to answer. He was in his car, turning the ignition, before he could answer. "I don't know," he said to the steering wheel, "sometimes you just got to. What the hell would life be like if all there was was white wine? Boy, do I got to get some food in me . . . boyohboy."

Balzic drove very carefully around the side streets and alleys of Rocksburg for twenty minutes and stopped in one of the small mom-and-pop restaurants in the flats by the river to get a large container of coffee to take with him. He hoped this particular mom and pop didn't know him, but they probably did and they were probably saying that cops couldn't catch all the criminals because the cops were all too busy making their lips purple. Balzic resolved to start listening to his wife and to never drink anything but white wine during working hours.

He heaved himself back into the car and knew an instant too late that he had sat on the foil-wrapped sandwich. In his haste to lift himself off the sandwich, he knocked over the plastic foam cup in his lap. Before he remembered that the cup had a lid tightly affixed to it, he lurched to catch the cup and jammed his thumb against the steering wheel hard enough to tear a corner of the nail away from the flesh.

"Goddamn!" he howled and sucked his wounded thumb. "I gotta quit drinking so goddamn much."

He was moaning, sucking on the thumb, cursing himself for his seeming inability to know when he'd had enough wine, and trying to reach under his rump to salvage the sandwich when he felt somebody standing by the still-open door of his car.

His head jerked about.

There, looking more ill at ease than befuddled — and he was befuddled — was rookie Patrolman Gregory Yurisich. He had been a patrolman for only three months and had just days ago finished his two-week training with the state police.

"Sir," Yurisich said, after clearing his throat. "Sir, can I be of any assistance?"

Balzic removed his throbbing thumb from his mouth with as much dignity as he could muster.

"Yeah," Balzic said, trying hard to not slur his words. "Yeah, you got a Band-Aid? I almost tore my goddamn thumbnail off here."

"Yes, sir, I got the first-aid kit in my cruiser." Yurisich sprinted away.

Balzic thrust his pelvis upward, rescued the sandwich and tucked it safely on the dashboard, then pried the lid off the coffee cup and drank three long swallows. The coffee was in his stomach before he realized that he had just scalded a layer of skin off the roof of his mouth. He didn't care. He had to get something in him that would at least begin to counteract the wine.

He leaned back in the seat and closed his eyes. "Of all goddamn times this kid gotta find me . . ."

When the rookie patrolman returned, eager to present three different-sized adhesive bandages, Balzic said, "Yurisich, what the hell're you doing here anyway?"

"Sir?"

"Knock off the 'sir' crap and tell me what you're doin' here."

"Uh, sir, this is my beat."

Balzic felt himself swallow and sigh and then he said, holding out his good hand for the bandages, "Yeah, I guess it would be. Well, go on and work it."

"Yes, sir," Yurisich said, dropping the bandages in Balzic's hand and taking two quick steps backward.

"And quit all the goddamn sirs. This ain't the Pentagon. Well? Go on, get outta here." Balzic pulled the door shut and went to work on his thumb, using his teeth to get one of the bandages open and pull its backing off. Awkward as it was, he got the bandage in place. He started the car and put it in gear before he remembered where he'd put the coffee and then succeeded, by some dexterity he could not have explained, to catch the cup before it fell off the dash, spilling only one tiny splash on his hand. It was still scalding hot.

He expelled another long, noisy sigh and drove off toward the station at a speed so slow that two drivers laid on their horns while passing him. One driver, a woman, thrust her right hand at him with the middle finger up. He saluted her with the plastic foam cup.

The other driver, a man long ago retired, flashed his false teeth at Balzic in a glare so full of strength and justification that Balzic did nothing but shrug meekly in return. There was no point in spoiling what would doubtless happen less and less for the old man. Balzic hoped that when his teeth were clacking together because his gums were shriveling he could blow his horn and pass somebody half his age and still have wits enough to remember why a glare would be a fitting thing to do.

Balzic turned carefully into the parking lot behind City Hall and thought, I'll pass some asshole with my teeth floppin' around and give him that kind of look and it'll be my luck he has a shotgun and blows my trunk off.

Balzic eased into his parking slot, the one with his nameplate fixed to the side of the building, and hit the building just hard enough to dump the plastic foam cup off the dashboard, where he'd just set it down, onto his right leg.

His scream brought Patrolman John Petrolac and Desk Sergeant Vic Stramsky out of the station house with their side arms drawn.

Balzic was out of his car, hopping on his left foot and swearing at Stramsky and Petrolac.

"Put those guns away! I just spilled coffee on myself, that's all! Get those guns away from me! Nothing's wrong, I just burnt myself. You two listenin'? Nobody's out here but me! Put those fuckin' guns away before we all get hurt!"

Stramsky looked knowingly at Petrolac. "I told you it was goin' to be one of those nights. The first really stinking hot night of the year and you can bet on it every time. I never —"

"Oh quit philosophizing for crissake and c'mere and take a look at my leg, see if I gotta go to the emergency room." Balzic pulled up his pant leg. "Come on! Take a look. I'm not jokin'. I dumped a pint of coffee on me and it was smokin'."

Stramsky holstered his weapon and got down on his haunches to look at Balzic's leg. "Well, you can go to the emergency room if you want to, but I don't think you have to. Your leg's not even red."

"It's not?"

Stramsky shook his head no and stood up. "Boy, your eyes are, though."

"Oh, you sound like a trained observer," Balzic said. "I'll bet you're a police officer or something." He pushed the wet pant leg down from above his knee and started in to the squad room of the station.

It remained for Stramsky to shut the car's engine off, turn out the lights, take the keys, and close the door.

"Now what're all these calls about?" Balzic said over his shoulder, holding up the three notes his wife had given him at home.

Stramsky and Petrolac followed Balzic in and watched him rummage through desk drawers apparently trying to find a coffee cup. Stramsky motioned to Petrolac to get Balzic some coffee.

"Some woman's going crazy 'cause we're not doing nothing about finding her husband. She's really pitching a bitch. Says if we don't do something — and right — fast, she's gonna sue everybody's ass for so much she's gonna own the town and everybody in it, especially us just so she can fire us all."

"Her name's Romanelli, right?"

"Right. How'd you —"

"Well, earlier, right after the all-day bullshit and right before this bullshit, there was a time when I almost felt like an ordinary person, just sitting and sipping my Robert Mondavi and this little girl calls Muscotti's and throws everything out of joint."

"Oh. Well, if I'd've known you knew about it I wouldn't've bothered you."

"You send anybody to talk to her or her neighbors?"

"Yeah. Petrolac went down."

"Well?"

Petrolac appeared then at Balzic's side and handed him a ceramic mug of coffee. "She wouldn't talk to me," Petrolac said. "Watch it, this stuff's really hot."

"Well, she must've said something."

"All she said was she wasn't gonna talk to no goddamn patrol-man. She wanted to talk to the chief. And that's the way she said it, too."

Balzic blew on his coffee. "Uh-huh. And what'd the neighbors say?"

"Well," Petrolac said, nodding to Stramsky, "he don't think there's anything wrong, but all those people, on every side of her, as soon as I mentioned her name, they just went silent. Then they'd start to mumble about how they didn't know them and how the two of them kept pretty much to themselves and all that."

"You think there's something wrong?"

Petrolac nodded.

Stramsky snorted. "Shit, he's probably shacked up some-place —"

"Well why would the neighbors dummy up like that?" Petro-lac said.

"Did they dummy up or did you think they dummied up or did you come on too strong?" Stramsky said.

"I didn't come on too strong and I didn't imagine it either. I talked to people in four different houses. They all knew him, and her too, and they just, I'm tellin' you they just — ah, I don't know. Maybe I asked them wrong, but they quit . . ." Petrolac shrugged as his voice trailed off.

"Don't worry about it," Balzic said, patting Petrolac on the shoulder. "You should've seen me when I first started. Used to use the wrong tone, the wrong face, I'd stand wrong. Hell I did everything to get people all out of joint and never knew I was doing it. Oh, I really screwed some things around. You let me get some of this — what is this stuff anyway? God it's awful stuff. Anyway, soon as I get enough of this gup in me to qualify as a wide-awake drunk we'll go talk to the lady again and you can see how it's done.

"The trick is looking like there's something wrong with you, like you got a hernia or something or a bad back or one leg shorter than the other, anything to make 'em think you can't hurt 'em. Shit, they'll tell you anything. You got to know when to look weak, Petrolac. And you got to know how. You got to practice — hey, I'm not kiddin' — you got to get a full-length mirror and practice looking mean and practice even more how to look like a goddamn crippled altar boy.

"Hey, boy, you're young and you got a lot of bad road ahead, but the worst are always the fuckin' DD, domestic disturbances, partner. You got to know how to roll over on your back and show your throat. 'Cause if you don't know that, one of 'em'll tear your throat out anyway. You got to study the animals and see how they surrender without givin' up. It's not easy to learn. A lotta guys can't bring themselves to do it. They just can't quit riding their balls around. And they go into somebody's kitchen and the venom and the sweat's flyin', never mind what else, and they can't park their balls outside, well, somebody's gonna get hurt. That's when the shit flies and the blood flows and once I had to tell a lady she was no longer a wife and I'll tell you there ain't nothin' worse than that last job. Nothing."

Balzic had drunk two cups of awful coffee while he'd been talking and had chased them with two cups of ice water and he was almost beginning to feel human again.

"Well, let's go see Mrs. Romanelli, Petrolac. You drive. I've had enough of that shit today."

They had been driving for ten minutes before Petrolac blurted out, "Why you have to be a cripple?"

Balzic, whose mind had been rummaging over an incoherent group of ideas, emotions, and obligations, looked at Petrolac as though he didn't know him or where they were going or why. Petrolac took Balzic's expression to mean that he hadn't heard the question.

"Why do you have to be a cripple when you ask questions?"

"Huh? Oh no. No. You don't have to *be* a cripple. You have to *look* harmless. And the easiest way to *look* harmless — the psychological shorthand you give people, get it? — is to make them think you been wounded in a way that makes them feel good that they weren't.

"I admit, that's hard to do when you're wearing that uniform and that badge and carrying heat. I mean, everything you represent — again in psychological shorthand — is 'mean daddy.' 'Bad poppa.' You ain't 'justice,' or the symbol of authority or whatever, you're plain old 'bad dad' coming to take names and whip asses.

"Now a lotta people love that. They love talking to 'bad dad.' Those ones — they'll beat your ears to death. But they're useless. They just want to get their ass whipped and when they find out you're not there to do it, then they get in a pout and you realize you been wastin' your time.

"Whatsamatter, Petrolac," Balzic said, "did it gall you when I said you had to show them your throat?"

"No, no. That's not it. It's just that's not what we were told at the state police school."

"What'd they tell you — make everybody else sit down, huh? And don't ever slouch, huh? Shit. If the state guys could wear stilts, they would. Hell, they never take those Smokey Bear hats off. Makes 'em feel half a foot taller.

"Shit, why do you think MacArthur had all the guys on that battleship in Tokyo Bay over six feet tall? Hell, when those little Japs came on board to sign that surrender paper, they had to look up at every face on that ship. You think they didn't feel whipped?"

Since Petrolac hadn't been born until two years after the Japanese surrendered on a battleship in Tokyo Bay to end World War II, he had no idea what Balzic was talking about. He wasn't even sure he knew who MacArthur was.

"But, Petrolac, my boy, in a DD you don't have people coming onto your ship to look up to you and see what a big, bad, mean man you are. You're goin' into their domicile, their residence, I don't care if it's a tarpaper shack, it's theirs, and nineteen times out of twenty they got to stop fighting to come see who's at the door. Then they got to unlock it, and then they got to stand aside.

"Now what'd the state guys tell you to do right then — step right in, right? And stand tall and talk in an au-thor-i-ta-tive voice, right?"

"Yeah, right."

"Petrolac, that's why so many women who used to be married to state cops are collectin' widows' pensions. 'Cause, boy, right there, when that door opens, what you better do is take off your hat and put both hands on it so they can see you ain't holding a gun or a stick and the first word out of your mouth better be 'may,' as in 'May I come in please?' "

"Well, what if, well, what if they say no, or fuck you, or who called you, or get the fuck off my steps — then what?"

"Then you look 'em right in the eye and you say it again. 'May I come in please?' Slow and clear. And never lose eye contact."

"And what if they still tell me to go to hell or get lost?"

"You say it again. And if you got the same question, I'm goin' to give you the same answer. You say it again. You make them focus on that one issue, whether or not you may come in. Petrolac, I've never had to say it more than four times."

"And nobody ever got crazy or violent?"

"I didn't say that. Lots of 'em got crazy and violent. All I'm sayin' is that lots of others who would've got crazy didn't because I didn't."

"But what about the ones who got crazy?"

"Oh well shit, of course, then I got crazy back. You have to protect yourself."

Petrolac looked immeasurably relieved, as though a thing precious to him that he feared might be lost forever was not lost at all but was, in truth, right where it had always been.

"But, Petrolac, the point is, double D is the worst. There isn't anything worse because you're dealing with pure emotion. Almost one hundred percent pure. There's a fire goin' on and the last thing it needs is a guy in a uniform with a mouthful of gasoline looking like he's gettin' ready to spit."

Balzic felt the car come to a halt off the berm of a narrow asphalt street.

"Where the hell are we?" Balzic said. As was usual when he had been drinking too much, he had been giving a lecture. He had been giving one for a long time, and in giving it he had been concentrating on what he was going to say so much that he ignored where the car had been driven or where it was now.

"Kennedy Township," Petrolac said. "I thought you knew this woman."

"No. I know her father. I don't know — I haven't seen her for years. Hell, she was a little girl." Balzic wondered why he was so touchy about knowing this girl that he was almost saying he didn't know her. He looked at the small clapboard houses on both sides of the street.

They were in one of the hundreds of coal patches in Conemaugh County, all built in the late nineteenth and early twentieth centuries when deep mining for bituminous coal was second only to farming as an industry. This patch, Kennedy Township, was incorporated as a township rather than a village only because some earlier inhabitant had gotten political ambitions, more likely for himself than for his village, and had persuaded enough of his neighbors to agree with him that their patch ought to be called a township instead of a village. He probably was among the first elected supervisors.

Whatever the coal patches were called now — company towns, villages, townships, patches — there were two major differences from what they had been. Now, the houses were privately owned because, now, there was no more coal coming out of the ground. It was easy enough to recognize those two facts. What was not easy to recognize was the change of attitude over the generations about who owned the property and how it was to be cared for, both financially and physically.

Balzic glanced around in the rapidly failing light of dusk. Across the street was a house with three cars parked on the grass, two on one side and one on the other — all the cars six to eight years old, all with their rear ends higher than their fronts, with dual exhaust pipes and wide tires with white lettering on the sidewalls, and with body colors that ranged from the seemingly careless gray of primer paint to the outrageous sheen of metalflake orange or yellow. Balzic could not be sure of the colors. One thing he was sure of: the house sandwiched between the cars seemed on the verge of collapse.

The houses on the near side — Petrolac had parked between two of them — were painted white and surrounded by flowers. The architecture of all the houses was identical; they had, after all, been built by a coal company and the ideas behind them had been speed and ease of construction. But sometime in the last twenty years the coal had veined-out or the shafts had flooded, and the company left to seek other veins.

What followed was an advance by what were politely called speculators, individuals and small real estate companies, who offered solid terms aimed to appeal to the coal company's sense of easy escape. The miners who had just lost their jobs then learned that they were about to lose their homes. More than one real estate speculator lost blood when he appeared with the first notices of the change of title and the terms under which the occupants might retain their residences. Very quickly, the speculators learned never to appear unarmed or unaccompanied by at least one constable or deputy sheriff, preferably both.

Life in the patches in the 1950s was at times as exciting as it had been in the early days of union organizing.

Many things could and did change about the patches, but there was this one constant: if a miner managed by some luck to gain title to the house he occupied while he was indebted both in salary and in labor to the company that had departed and left him to the mercy of the speculators, that miner cared for the house as though it were his second mother, one that he had chosen and one that he could care for from without as from within. And care for her he did. He painted her, puttied her, shingled her roof, caulked her crevices, and manicured her grounds. He doted on her, and pity the ignorant fool who approached her indifferent to the labor she required or to the esteem in which both she and the labor were held.

Balzic knew many miners who fit that description. Most of them were retired. He knew something else about them. Somewhere near the doors of their houses, both front and back, were a shotgun or a pick handle or both. It was as though these men couldn't get out of the habit. What's more, and Balzic knew this too, if a visitor didn't knock on one of these doors with respect for this knowledge, then he shouldn't be knocking at all.

"Uh, Chief, what're we waiting on?"

"Huh? Nothin', nothin', just tryin' to get a little oxygen in me. Takin' some deep breaths over here, that's all. Which house?"

"The one on your right."

"Well, let's get on with it."

They walked some fifteen feet over a recently poured concrete walkway. And then onto a small square porch. There was an aluminum storm door and to the right was a small wooden starburst with the name painted in white letters: Romanelli.

Before Balzic could look around further or knock, the inner wooden door was pulled open suddenly and there, confronting him, was a short, wiry bird of a woman with long black hair pulled severely away from her face.

He didn't know what he'd expected to see, but her presence threw him. She didn't look like her father, and Balzic couldn't remember what her mother had looked like. He began to think that he'd probably expected to see a little girl, a toddler, as though time had frozen. She wore a white, sleeveless, nondescript blouse, and a blue wraparound skirt that tied in the front. She was holding both a cigarette and a glass with some clear liquid in her right hand. She wore no makeup, though Balzic doubted if there were any cosmetics sold that could have covered the massive bruise on her left cheek. It spread to her nose, her eyebrow, and very near to her ear.

She could have been twenty or forty — she had that kind of face, complexion, and figure. She glanced quickly from Balzic to Petrolac and back, and, without a word, she pushed open the screen door a few inches and then stepped back away from it as Balzic caught the door thrust toward him, opened it, and stepped inside.

Whatever had been her emotions earlier when she'd been talking to Vinnie and Balzic, she now seemed to have herself in control. Balzic wondered if she was perhaps just a little drunk. In any case, there was not a glimmer of recognition on her part. She may as well have been looking at a wall.

"Uh, Mrs. Romanelli, you mind very much if I sit down? I hurt my back yesterday and, uh, I'm —"

"Help yourself." She nodded and then pointed to the couch and then changed her mind. She stepped over to an old wooden rocker. "Use this chair. It's the one Jimmy uses all the time. He's got a real bad back. You want some aspirin? Jimmy takes about ten a day."

"No, no thanks. I just took a couple." Balzic eased himself into the rocker and glanced quickly around the room. It was a large room, but Balzic knew from having been in these patch houses that there was only one other room on this level and that was the kitchen. This room was dining room, living room, TV room, home office, card room, and party room on the holidays all in one.

The furniture matched — except for the rocker Balzic was sitting in — and probably came from a discount house that dealt exclusively in styles guaranteed not to satisfy anybody's taste. It didn't have a name, this style of furniture. All one could be sure of, Balzic guessed, was that no doctor or dentist would want it for his waiting room. Other than that, the most that could be said for it was that the tables at either end of the couch looked alike and so did the fabric on the couch, the chair, and the ottoman. The six chairs surrounding the Formica-covered table at the far end of the room also matched. Taken collectively, the furniture had the look of having been bought because the price was right and not because it was part of a larger scheme.

Aside from cheap copies of wintry landscapes and still lifes of fruit and flowers on the walls, the only object to disrupt the tone of the room was the mounted head of a white-tailed deer on the wall above the dining area. The buck's rack of antlers had eleven points. Balzic looked at it for a moment, wondering how taxidermists managed to always get that waxy-eyed majesty in a deer's head. Maybe "waxy-eyed majesty" wasn't the right phrase for what taxidermists achieved, but there was something both mild and maniacal to Balzic about the eyes of a mounted deer's head.

Balzic ritually hunted deer for years even though he knew from the first moment he ever saw one that he would never shoot it and had indeed never fired a bullet within three feet of one except to scare it because he knew other hunters were nearby.

Balzic had nothing against hunters in general — he had hunted birds all his adult life — or deer hunters in particular. There was something he just couldn't understand about boasting about it, and having a deer's head mounted and left on a wall was a boast without end. It reminded Balzic of a marine he'd met coming back to San Francisco after World War II. The marine had an envelope in his wallet and in the envelope was a strand of pubic hair from every female who'd allowed him to bed her. It was a meager collection, but the marine was extremely proud of it and Balzic could not think of him without a special sadness. Balzic could not explain why. It was just sad.

"Jimmy killed that the season before last."

"Huh? Oh, the deer."

"I never saw Jimmy that happy."

"The day he killed him?"

"No," she said slowly, "the day he brought that home and put it up."

"Well, I guess it was a pretty important day," Balzic said, trying to get a good look at the bruise on Mrs. Romanelli's face. She kept turning her face away from him each time she saw him looking at her.

"Mrs. Romanelli, do you, uh, remember me?"

"No. Am I supposed to?"

"Well, it was a long time ago, I was in high school and you were a little girl and, uh, your father and my father used to be pretty good friends. I remember coming out to your father's house with my father. It's been a lot of years, but I used to watch you when they were playing cards and drinking wine and eating those hand grenades, those cherry peppers? You remember any of that? Huh?"

"My father still does that, how could I forget?" She thought a moment. "But I don't remember what you're talking about. I must've been pretty little."

"Oh you were. You were just a toddler. And my dad and your dad would sit out back under the grape arbor — remember that?"

"He still sits out there."

"And they'd drink wine and eat those hand grenades. Man, Petrolac, d'you ever eat them? They get halfway to your stomach and then they go off in your mouth. Man oh man, what heat comes out of those little vegetables."

"This is all very nice," Mrs. Romanelli said, sighing too loudly, "but what do you have to tell me about my husband? I mean I know where my father is. He's two doors down where he's been for God knows how many years. What about my husband?"

"Mrs. Romanelli, uh, Frances, may I call you Frances?"

"Who cares? Call me Frances if it makes you happy." She lurched way from the dining room table, which she'd been leaning against, and began to pace.

"Uh, Frances, why don't you sit down and tell me about what's going on. Uh, Petrolac, do me a favor and get me a glass of water in the kitchen, okay, huh, go on, that's it."

"The glasses are above the sink on your right," Frances said, looking at the floor and rubbing the bridge of her nose. She darted quickly to the table at the far end of the couch and stabbed out another cigarette. In seconds, she was lighting another.

"Well, Frances, huh, you want to tell me? Okay?" Balzic slouched in the seat as low as he could. He put his right shoe on the edge of his left and began to rock his right knee back and forth the way a child would.

"Tell you what? I told you. On the phone. I haven't seen my husband since yesterday morning. He called me yesterday from that bar he always goes to —"

"Muscotti's?"

"Yeah. And he said he was going to have another beer and be on his way."

"Yeah, well, uh, Frances, I know that much, but what about the rest? Huh?"

Petrolac was standing awkwardly at Balzic's side with the water Balzic had asked him to get. Now Balzic seemed not to care
that Petrolac had gotten it.

"What rest? The rest of what?"

Balzic took the glass of water from Petrolac and said, "Frances,
you know those aspirin you asked me if I wanted, huh? I think
maybe I better take them, if you'll get them for me, please, okay?
The ones I took aren't doing the job."

"Huh? Oh. Aspirins. Sure."

"Would you please? I'd really appreciate it." Balzic looked at
Petrolac and whispered after she'd stepped past them to go into
the kitchen, "You paying attention? I'm working my ass off
here, I hope you're taking some notes. Fuckin' guys get Oscars
in Hollywood for stuff that ain't half as good as I'm doing here.
I mean, observe the feet and the posture. This is the way a little
kid sits. You ever study that, huh? Hey, Petrolac, askin' questions ain't all hitting wise guys in the head with a Pittsburgh
phone book, you know?"

Petrolac was going to reply, but instead indicated with his eyes
that Mrs. Romanelli was returning with the aspirin.

"How many do you want?" she said.

"Two's okay."

She held them out and Balzic took them in his hand and swallowed them with water with a motion resembling a bird drinking, throwing his head back several times after each swallow.

"Hey, thank you very much. I think this is going to be all
right now." He looked up at her over his glasses and under his
brows and said, "Now, what's going on here lately? I know you
two have been having some trouble here, but what's it all about?
Now why would he want to hurt you and just leave like that
and not tell you where he was going? That's not right to worry
you like that."

She looked at Balzic for a time as though she could not believe
what she was hearing, and then she just seemed to crumple and
sat on the couch, her forehead in her hand, and she shook her
head from side to side for nearly a minute and fought back tears.

"Jimmy's not the same," she began. "He used to be the best

guy, the best person I ever knew. And then the mine shut down. And it was like . . . there was nothing I could say that made it any better. It was like everything I said or did made it worse."

She stopped to collect her thoughts and then she shot a mistrustful glance at Balzic, as though she knew positively that he would not be able to understand what she was about to say and that she was being very foolish for even thinking about saying it.

"He's not the same," Balzic said, "but he still never stayed away this long, right?"

She nodded slowly.

"He ever hit you before?"

"He's never hit me," she said sharply. "My father did this."

Balzic shifted about on the rocking chair and tried to find something to look at so it wouldn't appear obvious how much of a lie he knew that last statement to be.

"Why'd your father hit you?"

"It doesn't make any difference," she said. "We're getting off the subject."

"Yeah, I guess we are. So why'd he take off on you like that?" Balzic almost smiled. Sometimes when he was halfway between drunkenness and soberness he could come up with a question just full of enough contradictions and ambiguities that it seemed to be going in opposite directions from where he'd been when in fact he'd never left where he was.

"I don't understand that question," she said.

Shit, Balzic thought. So much for halfway between drunken and sober genius.

"Oh, forget it," Balzic said. "Just tell me about your husband. What he does, where he goes, who he goes with, and who he does it with."

"That's just it," Frances said. "Since the mine closed, I don't know who he's doing anything with or where. And it's getting worse, it's gotten a lot worse in the last five or six months."

"How long since he worked?"

"Fourteen months," she said without hesitation.

"When'd the checks run out?"

"Two months ago."

"What didn't the checks cover?"

"What didn't they? Uh, it'd be easier to say what they did cover. All they covered was the mortgage on the cabin we had by the reservoir."

Balzic slouched even lower in the rocking chair. "What'd you have to sell? D'you have to sell some things, huh?"

She sighed and shook her head slowly and stared wistfully at the floor. "The boat. Then we made a deal on the car and the pickup. The guy took over the payments and gave us his car. We really took a beating on that, but we would've lost them both and everything we put into them if we didn't do it like that. God, he cried when the guy drove the pickup away. I mean real tears in his eyes. You know, the only time Jimmy was ever off work was when there was a strike. Jimmy always had money.

"It killed him to sign up for his check every week. Killed him. He had to get half-blasted to do it.

"And, oh my God," she said, shaking her head with her eyes closed, "when I told him we were eligible for food stamps, I thought he was gonna die. I mean it. He got all white and he started to sweat. He looked like hell. And he said his fingers got numb."

"Did he do it?"

"Sign up for food stamps?"

"Yeah. Did he or did you?"

"I did. He tried, he really did. But he couldn't do it. He said the questions they asked him and the way they talked to him down the public welfare office made him feel like he knew how niggers felt. He got sick when he came home. I mean really sick, you know, throwing up and he got a fever and, oh my God, he looked like hell."

"So, uh, when'd you go back to work?"

"I never said I did."

"Well, somebody had to. You're still living here." Balzic said it so softly she had to lean forward to hear him.

"Well, my father couldn't keep helping us. And Jimmy's parents died a long time ago. He's the only son. He doesn't have any brothers. And his sisters aren't going to help him. He wouldn't even think of asking them."

"How many sisters does he have?"

"Three."

"Married?"

She nodded. "Laverne's married to a plumber, Rose is married to a carpenter, and Sylvia's married to a roofer. They all got good jobs."

"Any of the brothers-in-law offer to help out?"

She looked at him as though he were crazy. "Are you kiddin' me? What was Jimmy supposed to do if they did? Take it? Huh? Jesus Christ, he could never look his sisters in the face again."

Balzic said nothing for a long moment. He continued to look at her as though she had more to say and he was not going to interrupt her until she said it. He hoped Petrolac was paying attention.

"Well, I mean, if he got hurt or something, you know, lost a leg or got paralyzed, then it would've been okay for his sisters to help him out." She paused and studied Balzic's face. "You know what I'm talking about?"

Balzic nodded.

"I mean if he's hurt that's okay. But he's not hurt or nothing, so he got to, uh, well, you know."

"I know," Balzic said. "If he's got his health he's got to make his wealth, right?"

She lit another cigarette and blew out a mouthful of smoke. "Yeah! Right. That's it, that's it exactly." She sighed and shook her head. "It's so stupid. I mean, Jesus, can anything be stupider than that?"

She stood up and began to pace from the couch to the dining table and back, slowly, pacing and speaking as though this was the very first time she was saying some things in her own home that she had been thinking about for a long time but had never dared to say.

"I mean, never once did they ever come over here to see if we needed anything. Not once. I mean I know his sisters. But you'd've thought at least once one of them would've come over and said, 'Hey, you eating okay? You got soap to wash clothes? You got gas for the car?' No sir. Not once in fourteen months. It was like we had black lung and they didn't want to listen to us breathe.

"If it wasn't for my father before I went to work we'd've starved to death. My father gave us twenty-five dollars every week for food until I got my first pay. He even paid for all my refresher courses at the community college.

"Refresher. That's a laugh. I didn't remember a thing from high school. And, oh brother, what I never knew when I took those courses, I mean, never mind what I forgot, I mean all the stuff I had to learn, Jee-suss."

"That wasn't in the books, huh?" Balzic said.

"Oh, right. Oh, believe me. Right. That's when, I mean, when I look back at it now, that's when Jimmy really started to get crazy."

"Why should you be any different from his sisters, right?" Balzic said, peeling off the Band-Aid on his thumb and trying to appear indifferent to his own question.

"Yeah. Right! That was exactly it! Why should I be different from them? They never went to college, so who'd I think I was? They never thought about no job, so what the hell was I doing gettin' a job? They stayed home and took care of what they were supposed to take care of, so how come I wasn't?

"And I listened to that for about two months and finally this lady I met at the college, we started having coffee together every day, and I told her about this and she said why didn't I tell him that his precious sisters, they could afford to stay home because their old man didn't get laid off, not one of them, they were all still working and the reason I was going to college was I was tired of taking handouts from my father when there was nothing wrong with you — meaning Jimmy —" She stopped pacing and clapped her hand over her mouth to stifle what sounded like a laugh and a sob together. "Oh Christ, what a jerk I was."

"Why?" Balzic asked softly.

"Why? Hell, don't you know? Can't you guess?"

Balzic knew at once but he waited for her to say it.

" 'Cause I did it. I came right home that day and I did it. Said it just like she said without thinking about it because I knew if I thought about it I'd never say it.

"Godohgod what a mistake that was. I think it would've been easier on Jimmy if I'd've taken one of his guns and tried to shoot him." She shook her head for a long time.

"And after that it really started to go downhill, huh?"

Her eyes filled up with tears. She put her hand to her mouth and then tried to press her lips together to keep herself from sobbing out loud.

"Downhill?" She let out a long sigh. "There isn't a word for where we went. Off the hill I think. Yeah. We went down so fast we went clear off the hill.

"You know," she went on, but in a different tone now, less caustic, more reflective, "I kept taking my classes and picking up the typing real fast — it really came back to me fast, not the shorthand though, I mean I really stink at shorthand — and I kept talking to my friend between classes and the next thing I know I got two part-time jobs that almost add up to thirty hours a week, nothing great, you know, the minimum wage, but it's not a handout, and I'm really starting to like it, 'cause I never done it before, not in my whole — I gotta quit saying 'done it' 'cause that's incorrect and I'm never going to get any kind of job if I can't at least use halfway decent grammar, you know, I mean, Jee-suss, part-time work's nice, but it's still part-time — where was I?"

"You were starting to like it," Balzic said.

"Huh? Oh yeah. But — but I was also starting to hate it. I mean, I'd love it as long as I was doing it, but then about a half hour before quitting time I'd start thinking about Jimmy and what he's gonna look like, what's his face gonna look like, and then I'd really start to hate myself for liking what I was doing so much. Jee-suss, I never felt guilty in my life, not for anything, I mean, I used to wonder what in the hell people were talking about when they were talking about feeling guilty and I never knew. I mean, I never knew!

"But I sure found out. I mean, I had a bad conscience some times. Lots of times. But nothing like this! I mean, it was really a heavy thing. Honest to God, a weight. I could feel it just coming down on my neck and shoulders right before I'd come home. And the closer I'd get to the house the worse it'd get. One night I got out of the car and I almost couldn't straighten up. It was a joke! Oh my aching back. How many times people say that. How many times you hear it? I thought it was baloney." She shook her head forcefully from side to side. "It is definitely not baloney. Something weighs on your mind, it starts to weigh on your back, honest to God it does. And if you can't find some way to get rid of it, it'll break your back. I'm serious! It will!"

Balzic nodded his head sympathetically. "Uh, you, uh, were doing other things at the community college?"

"Other things? Like what things?"

"Oh, like talking to other women like yourself. Like maybe sitting around and, you know, doing a little shop talk back and forth, seeing how you're doing, each other, huh?"

"Oh yeah. There's a regular program there for women who never had to work before. Oh yeah. For women like me and widows and women whose kids grew up. And it's been so long since they had a job or they never had one, they don't know how to dress for a job interview." She was more animated now.

"Oh yeah, for a long time I thought they was a bunch of — uh, were a bunch of women's libbers or maybe worse, uh, you know, but it turned out they were only all like me. Well, you know, not like me, but we were all there with the same reasons. More or less. And you know what was funny? Huh? We were all scared shitless. Excuse my language, but it's true. We were.

"We'd get in our discussion groups, you know, where we'd all sit around and each one would talk about their problems and for the first couple of weeks there were more of us in the lavatory than there was in the — is that, no that should be — there *were* in the room."

Frances stopped and took a deep breath and looked at Balzic, slouched low in the rocker, and Petrolac, standing with his hands folded behind his back and leaning against the wall opposite her,

and looked at their faces back and forth. After a long moment of
looking back and forth she said, "This is crazy. This is really
crazy. Do you know that I'm telling you things, you two guys,
one I never seen — saw — before in my life and the other one,
you, who says I'm — says? — you used to watch me when I was
little and I'm telling you things that have got me —" She broke
off abruptly.

"Things that have got you what?" Balzic said. "Punched?"

"Punched?" She tried to laugh but no sound came out. "That's
a good one. If that's all — I mean, I wished that's what did happen
most of the time instead of what does. I mean, except when it
does. When I get punched. Then I think I would rather have the
other stuff."

"What other stuff?"

She was drawing back into herself now. Balzic could see it because it was happening so fast she seemed almost to be occupy-
ing less space.

"What other stuff?" he asked again.

She shook her head as though she had just caught herself being very foolish for talking about herself and remembered what
grief was going to come to her for this foolishness. She stood up
and said, "I'm going to make some coffee. It's instant so it's no
trouble if you want some. I'll be happy to make it for you."

Damn, Balzic thought, she was really humming right along
there and now it's gone. And there wasn't a thing he could do
on this night to get her back. She might talk about other things,
but there'd be no more about these conflicts and, for that matter,
there might not be anything more about her still-missing husband. Balzic had to get her talking about that. And who knew,
Balzic thought, maybe she might get back on this.

"Hey, I could sure use a coffee, and so could my friend here,"
Balzic said, nodding in Petrolac's direction.

"Oh yeah. Sure. I'll have one too, long as you're making it,"
Petrolac piped up.

She said nothing as she got the pan, ran some water in it, put
it on one of the gas rings, and then got three cups, saucers, and

spoons and put the granules of instant coffee into each cup. She was absorbed in these small movements and actions, to the point of looking as though she had forgotten that anybody else was in the house with her. As Balzic observed her, his hope that she was going to talk about herself again slid away.

"Mrs. Romanelli, what about Jimmy?"

"What do you want to know?"

"What's he look like? Do you have a picture of him? Recent one would be better than any, but any would be better than none."

"The last pictures anybody took of Jimmy was — uh, oh shit — were in hunting camp when he killed that deer. They're in the drawer in the end table on the right end of the couch from where you're looking at it. He looks at those pictures a lot.

"You can go get them. There's nothing else in there except cards and poker chips and stuff. We used to play poker a lot. We don't do that anymore either, like a lot of other stuff we used to do."

Balzic motioned to Petrolac to get the pictures. Petrolac did and handed a stack of black-and-white snapshots to Balzic as Frances came out of the kitchen with two steaming cups of coffee and took them to the dining table at the far end of the room.

"Come on, sit here. I can't stand to see anybody jiggle hot coffee on his lap."

Balzic shot a quick glance at Petrolac, who was forcing down the corners of his mouth to keep from smiling. It was as Balzic suspected: Petrolac was having a good, quiet, private laugh over what had happened in the City Hall parking lot.

Frances went to the kitchen and returned with her coffee and an ashtray. "Don't neither of youns smoke? Oh crap, I gotta quit saying that too. God, all the stuff I gotta quit saying, I don't know if there's gonna be anything left I can say."

"You sound all right to me," Balzic said.

"Do I? Huh? I'm trying to be so careful, but every time I'd ask Jimmy if I was talking right, he'd say something snotty like why don't I go ask my 'college chums.' God, where he heard that expression, 'college chums,' I don't know, but it wasn't funny for very long."

"Oh, he probably heard it on a late movie on TV," Balzic said, now beginning to wonder if she'd open up again about herself.

"Anyway, you want to know about Jimmy. I'll tell you the God's truth, I'm really shook up. I never had these feelings before. Arguing's one thing. But when you think he's, uh, he's . . ."

"When you think something's happened to him?" Balzac said it just before he sipped his coffee and looked at Petrolac, but he watched her peripherally. He also pretended to look at the snapshots.

"Huh? No. I mean, yeah. You really get all screwed up in your mind about what you're supposed to feel and what you feel, I mean, really feel, and you don't know if you're just talking yourself into feeling something or if you're letting other people talk you into feeling things or if you — aw, Jeee-suss, I wish I knew what I know or whatever. Boy, that didn't make no sense at all. Any sense . . ."

She put her face in her hands and said, "God, I'm scared!" And she burst into tears and jumped up from the table and ran around the corner into the kitchen.

Balzic let her cry for almost a minute and then he went out and stood behind her. She was facing the refrigerator with her face in her hands and her hands pushed against the door and Balzic put his hands on her shoulders and said, "There, you go ahead, there. It's good to get that out, you just go ahead."

She stood there, sobbing for a minute or so, and then she turned away and went toward a box of tissues on a cabinet top near the sink. She pulled several tissues out of the box and wiped her eyes and blew her nose, staring at the wall and lost in thought.

"I wish I knew what happened," she said. "But that's dumb 'cause I know what happened. The mine closed. That's what happened. And I got tired of taking money from my father.

"And the trouble with Jimmy is he's only had two jobs since he got out of high school. The army and the mine. He got drafted into the army and his dad got him into the mine. Sounds crazy, but Jimmy's never had to ask nobody for nothing since he graduated from high school.

"He didn't even ask me to marry him. He just said, 'Let's get married,' and I said, 'Okay.' Just like that. . . . Jimmy can't ask people for anything. He just thinks it's his, like everybody's supposed to know what he wants and he don't — doesn't — even have to say what it is. And if you tell him maybe it would be a good idea for him to ask, he goes crazy. He gets all uptight and tries to turn it all on you.

"I mean, that was okay as long as he was working and we were buying whatever he wanted. Pffft! Here comes Jimmy with the paycheck. Pffft! Here comes Jimmy with a new idea for something to spend it on. Never asked me, never discussed it. It was his money, he earned it, he spent it. We'd go through the stuff in the supermarkets and I'd get to make all the decisions about what to buy but I never got to touch the money, no sir, nothing doing.

"And you know what? That's the way I liked it. I mean, it wasn't that's the way I liked it, it's that was the way it always was, so what was there for me not to like, huh?

"But then," she said, pausing to light still another cigarette, "the first time I get money from my father and we go to the store, I try to give it to him in the aisle before we go through the checkout line, and what do you think? He won't touch it. He puts his hands in his pockets and he turns his back on me and there I am, like a jerk, telling him, 'Here, Jimmy, take the money, please.' And what's he do? He walks away from me. He leaves me there. He walks out of the store and sits in the car.

"And you know what? Fourteen months since that happened, he ain't been back inside a grocery store with me since. Or any store. 'The person that makes the money spends the money,' that's what he says and there is nothing I can say and I mean *nothing* to get him to change his mind.

"But you know what else? He won't look for a job either."

Balzic found that hard to believe. "He won't even look for one?"

"Right hand to God and cross my heart on my mother's grave," she said, raising her right hand high and then making the sign of a cross over her heart with it.

"What about when he signed up for his unemployment?" Balzic said. "They had to find some jobs for him."

She shook her head and pursed her lips. "Every time they told him about a job, he'd say he was a miner, a coal miner, a bituminous coal miner, and he didn't have to take no job he wasn't qualified for. Now I don't know if that's baloney or not, I mean, when he first told me I believed him, but then he quit talking about what would happen down there and I don't know what to believe anymore."

"But, uh, there are mines around here," Balzic said.

"Sure there are. But according to him they were in Alaska. We'd have to move, we'd have to go through all the hassle of selling this place and our other place and buying another one and this and that and this and that — you know whose house this is? His parents' house. His mother left it to him. He's lived in this house all his life except when he was drafted in the army. I used to look at him and think what a man he was. Now, he gets laid off and all this other stuff comes out and I think, my God, I got the world's only forty-year-old baby for a husband.

"And that sounds really shitty, 'cause he took care of me all those years. I liked it the way he wanted it. It didn't bother me that I never touched the money, honest to God it didn't. But then I start to touch the money, first from my father and then what I'm making and it's like my money's dirt. I mean, if it isn't his way — Jimmy's — then it's nothing doing. We either do what he wants or we don't do nothing, period. Anything. It's crazy.

"And what makes it really crazy is I like doing what I'm doing. I like making money. It makes me feel good to go into a drugstore and buy a lipstick and not ask Jimmy whether I can have it. A lousy lipstick! D'you believe it? I couldn't buy a lousy lipstick without asking him and he'd go with me to the five-and-ten and I'd pick it out and we'd walk over to the clerk and he'd hand her the money and she'd say thank you to him and then I'd say thank you to him. And I liked that!"

"But now you like it the way you're doing it, huh?" Balzic said.

"Yeah! I do! And all Jimmy does is pout all goddamn day and he thinks I'm not having any trouble at all with the way we're living. I'm turning inside out! I'm thirty-six years old and I never had a job since I worked Christmas vacations in a department store over my last two years of high school and now all of a sudden I'm working two jobs and going to college and I'm still doing all the stuff I did when I didn't work and go to college. I still cook and clean and wash the clothes and, hell, now I even take the garbage out. Jimmy doesn't even do that anymore."

She shook her head and leaned against the kitchen wall and chewed a fingernail. Her eyes filled up again with tears. "What the hell's he want from me? I mean, what am I supposed to do? What else? He don't wanna — oh shit, forget that, I'm not going to talk about that. I mean, I'm not that far gone.

"Or maybe I am. You know what I got last week? Huh? Tranquilizers. Yeah. Variums or bariums or some screwy name —"

"Valiums," Balzic said.

"Yeah, them. That's right. Four a day I'm supposed to take, and you know what? I'm scared of them damn things. I took four the first day and two the next day and I fell asleep in class. Dead out! Now I don't know what to do. People tell me, take 'em, don't take 'em. The doctor says they won't hurt me, some woman in school says her sister got hooked on them, she's like a dope addict. I don't know what the hell I'm doing."

She threw up her hands and then put them on her head as though by that act she could keep her mind from spilling away from her.

"And now this," Balzic said.

"Right. And now this." She looked at Balzic squarely in the eyes. Her eyes had met his briefly many times before, but now she was fixing on him.

"You know, we must've really had something going when I was a little girl and you and your father used to come around here. I mean either that or you're a magician 'cause I can't even remember telling any of this stuff to . . ."

"I'm no magician," Balzic said. "We had something going. You were a pistol. Couldn't keep you from climbing things. Trees, fences, you'd crawl up on the cars. You were always up in the air somewhere. My dad used to tell your dad you were gonna be an aviator. Your dad used to laugh and say, sure, if you didn't break your neck before you learned how to count."

"Why'd you stop coming around?"

"My dad died. And then the war and I don't know why I never came back. Your dad lives two houses down, right? At the end of the street?"

"Yeah. You should go see him. He'd really like to see you I bet. Maybe you could get him to talk. He doesn't talk to anybody anymore. He won't talk to me. He's almost as bad as Jimmy."

"I thought you said he paid for your refresher courses."

"Oh, he did. But he never thought that was gonna mean that I'd wind up getting a job. Going to the community college was for just in case. And the 'just in case' was never supposed to happen. I mean, women don't work. Not jobs work. House work. That's all. He's been mad at me ever since I couldn't have kids. And now he thinks that the real reason I couldn't have kids — no, *didn't* have kids — was so I could eventually get a job. So now he thinks I lied to him about not being able to have kids. Honest to God, between Jimmy and my father, I can't win. I can't do anything right!

"I mean, here are the only two men in my life — no, not just men — the only two people in the whole world I care about and neither one of 'em'll talk to me and if Jimmy hadn't lost his job I'd've never found that out. I mean, imagine that! If that mine had never shut down and Jimmy would've never lost his job,

I'd've never found out what my father and my husband are really like.

"When I think of that, it drives me crazy. Sometimes I wake up in the middle of the night and I'm terrified, scared stiff, I can't get my breath — everything — and it's because I think not only my husband but also my father liked me a whole hell of a lot better when I was pretty much just a maid and a cook and a day worker. And I think, boy, they really thought a lot of me, didn't they? And these aren't some strangers, some people off the street, some perverts, these are my father and my husband. My father for thirty-six years. My husband for eighteen years.

"And in the last year, for all practical purposes, they both quit talking to me."

"And started punching you?" Balzic asked slowly.

"Yeah! Peace is over, brother, it's war around here. And I'm the enemy."

"Look, let's get one thing straight," Balzic said firmly. "I know that your father didn't do that to you. You want to keep telling me that, that's okay, but I know he didn't. I know I haven't seen him for a lot of years and everybody changes and all that, but I can't believe your father ever put a finger on your face. We understand one another about that cheek of yours now or not?"

She looked at the floor and then back up squarely into his eyes. "Okay," she said, but there was resignation in her tone and sorrow on her face. It was unmistakable to Balzic that she was agreeing only because disagreeing wouldn't be worth the trouble.

Balzic was so flustered by her reaction that he could think of nothing to do except go on as though he'd been right all along, that her father had never struck her, that only her husband had. Balzic felt very stupid; the moreso because he didn't know how to let her know that he knew. He was too shaken by this information about her father. It didn't fit with his ideas and memories about the man. He went on as though he hadn't learned anything.

"So when did this part of it start?"

"When else? When did everything else start around here?

The first time he came back from the unemployment office and they told him he had to go for this job interview and he came home and told me he wasn't going to do it — like I was the one making him. All I was trying to do was ask him to explain to me what they were telling him he had to do and, bam, he hit me with I don't know what 'cause I never saw anything coming and the next thing I knew I was on the floor and my whole head was ringing.

"After that, it just got to be a regular thing. We'd be having what I'd think was a sociable conversation and, whammo, there'd go the bells in my head.

"I just went out and bought the biggest pair of sunglasses I could find and prayed a lot that he wouldn't hit me in the mouth and break some teeth or knock 'em out. One thing about Jimmy, he's consistent. He manages to get me right on the cheekbone almost every time."

They both heard the footsteps at the same time and so did Petrolac. And then they all stood there looking at each other and at the door as a key went into the lock and turned and the door opened and there stepped into the room a short, thick, sweaty, fortyish man looking sheepish, bewildered, perplexed, and angry as his gaze went from his wife to Balzic to Petrolac and back to his wife.

He shut the door and started immediately to unbutton his white shirt and to pull it out of his trousers.

"So you went and did it, huh?" he said. "So you finally went and did it. I knew you would."

"Did what, Jimmy?" his wife said, "What'd I do? And before you tell me, ain't you gonna tell me anything else?"

"Ain't? Oh-ho. Ain't? You're slipping. What are your friends gonna think when they hear you giving out with the ain'ts? And no I ain't gonna tell you nothing else. These guys gonna arrest me?"

"Jimmy, I was worried. I didn't know —"

"Worried? My ass! Is that what you told them? Is that what she told you guys, huh? Worried? Shit, she don't know what worried means."

"Jimmy, for God's sake —"

"Uh, excuse me, Mrs. Romanelli," Balzic said. "Jimmy, my name's Mario Balzic, I'm chief of police —"

"I know who you are for crissake. What am I, stupid?"

"No. Nobody said you were. I was telling you who —"

"Well, I know who you are and I know who I am and I know who she is and him over there — I don't care who he is — but what the hell are youse all doing in my house since I didn't invite you? Huh?

"I mean, if youse are gonna arrest me then do it, and if not then get the hell out, okay? I mean one thing or the other but skip the bullshit. Okay?"

"Your wife was concerned about where you were and —"

"I said pass on the bullshit! Either arrest me for something or take a hike! This is my house, my name's on all the loans, I make the payments, and if I didn't break no law, then beat it! Get the hell outta my house! Just 'cause you're cops you can't walk right into people's houses —"

"I called them, Jimmy!" Frances said.

" 'Cause I wasn't here and you was worried, right?" he shot back at her. "Well, now I'm here and you can quit worrying. You called these guys in my house, right? Huh? Well then you can step outside and call 'em right back out. And don't give me no story. Don't talk to me about your reasons, or your emotions, or your whatever you been talkin' about lately. Just get 'em the hell outta my house! Now!"

"Take it easy, Jimmy," Balzic said.

"Hey, I already told you all I'm gonna say to you. Either arrest me or get lost. I don't wanna hear no speeches, no sermons, no nothing." He thrust his arms straight out in front of him with his fists close together. "Either put handcuffs on me right now or get out! And I don't care which one it is, but don't stand there yakkin' about it, okay?"

"I think we better all sit down and talk this over," Balzic said, walking slowly toward a chair near the dining table.

"We ain't talkin' nothin' over. What's the matter with you? Can't you hear me or something?" Jimmy said, following behind

Balzic. When Balzic sat down Jimmy looked at the table and saw the stack of snapshots of himself and his friends at the hunting camp during the season he'd shot the deer whose head was mounted on the wall.

"What the hell are — who the hell was looking through these? Huh?" He scooped them up and started immediately toward the table where Petrolac had found them. Jimmy opened the drawer and looked over his shoulder and waved the snapshots in a fury at Balzic and at his wife. "This is private, goddammit! This is mine. This is my privacy youse are messin' with here and you can't do that shit without a warrant or something. You can't just go poking your noses into people's privacy like that. Huh? What gives youse the right?"

"Jimmy, your wife said you'd been missing —"

"Missing? I wasn't missing. I knew right where I was the whole time."

"Yes, but she didn't and so she called because she was scared —"

"Scared? Sheeit, that's a good one."

"— because she was scared because this was not what you usually do —"

"What I usually do? What I usually do? I don't do nothing, that's what I usually do — didn't she tell you that? I ain't done nothing for fourteen months. My job quit. I didn't quit my job. My job quit me, there's a big difference."

"— because you don't usually leave for a whole day and a night and the rest of the next day," Balzic said, his patience wearing thinner by the word. "And so she called us and I asked her if she had a recent photograph of you because that is routine in the case where a person is reported missing. There was no invasion of —"

"But I wasn't missing. I ain't missing. Here I am. I'm right here, ain't I, Frances? Am I missing now, huh?"

Frances closed her eyes and shook her head and went back into the kitchen to run water over her cigarette to put it out and then to reach for another cigarette in the same motion.

"No, Jimmy, you're not missing." She turned to Balzic and

said, while rubbing her forehead with the heel of her hand, "I think you better go. Thanks for coming and, uh — just thanks."

"Anytime," Balzic said, standing and heading for the door, motioning for Petrolac to move right along out the door.

"Good night," Balzic called out as he pulled the door shut behind him.

Once outside, Balzic touched Petrolac's arm and motioned for him to wait a moment. A moment was all it took.

"You called the goddamn cops!" came Jimmy's voice.

"Because I was worried. Can't you understand that?"

"What the hell were you worrying about? You think I got hurt, huh? Something happened to me, huh? Since when'd you give a rat's ass?"

"Oh, Jimmy, honest to God —"

"You wanna know where I was, huh? Here, look, here's where I was. Making money. Look, here, count it. Here, go ahead, count it. There's a thousand bucks there — hey, wait a minute."

"What's the matter?"

"I didn't hear them cops start their car."

Balzic pulled Petrolac quickly and both made a dash up the short walk and onto the street, reaching the cruiser just as Jimmy pulled open his front door.

"D'you hear everything you wanted, youse cops, huh? You wanna know where I got the bread, huh? Playing cards, that's where. Go 'head and arrest me for that, too, youse clowns."

"C'mon, Petrolac, let's get out of here."

They were halfway back to the station before either of them said anything. Then Petrolac blurted out, "What a waste of time that was. Jeez."

"Waste of time? We didn't waste any time."

"We didn't waste time?" Petrolac said. "You mean that was good work there? All the time we were in that house listening to that woman bitch about her old man, we weren't wasting time?"

Balzic sighed. "Petrolac, I was giving — no, man, how can you say that? What the hell were you looking at? I was giving you the short course in handling one half of a domestic disturbance — maybe the most important half — and you, awww, shit, what'd you think I was doing there, feeding that lady's ego, huh? Throwing her a bone? Huh? Petrolac, didn't you hear that woman say that for all practical purposes her father and her husband have quit speaking to her on friendly terms?"

"Yeah. I heard."

"Well, what do you think you're supposed to do when somebody tells you something like that, huh?"

"I don't — I'm not sure I guess."

"Whatta you mean you guess you're not sure? Christ, man, that was half of a DD you were listening to. If that woman doesn't soon find somebody to talk to, that jerk of a husband of hers is gonna come home one night and belt her around and then sit down with his back to her and say something really intelligent like, 'Where's my dinner?' To which that lady is gonna look at the knives in the drawer, take out the longest one, close her eyes, and stick it clear through his chest from back to front."

Petrolac shook his head with the barest trace of a disbelieving smile on his face.

"You don't think so, huh?"

"No sir, I don't. I don't think she got the guts."

"Petrolac, guts doesn't have anything to do with it. What you heard in that house tonight was frustration, pure and simple. Fourteen months of it. That woman's had to turn her life upside down because her husband is still a little boy emotionally and she found it out after seventeen or eighteen years of being married to him. You know what that means, I mean one of the things it means?"

"I'm not sure I know what you're talking about."

"Well, among other things it means," Balzic said, "it means she misjudged the man she picked to be her husband. You know how you feel when you find out you've made a mistake? A serious mistake? You feel stupid."

"No, you don't — well, maybe you do, now that you mention it."

"Listen, Petrolac, you pay attention to this stuff because, I'm telling you, there ain't nothing you're ever going to be involved in that can get as hairy as walking in on a DD. And the more you know about how to cool people off the longer you're going to live, young fella, that's all there is to it."

"I understand what you're trying to tell me, Chief, I just think in this case, where we just came from, it was a big waste."

"Why? You tell me. I want to hear."

"Because look how fast she told us to leave to pacify him."

"Well, of course she did. Why's that make it a waste?"

"Because I think she likes getting smacked around."

"You do, huh? Well then, explain to me why this woman is working two jobs and going back to school at her age when she's never had to work since she got married and she got married right out of high school. I mean, does that sound or look like the actions of a woman who likes to get smacked around? Huh? Does that look like the actions of a woman who's gonna sit on her ass and not try to do anything to improve her situation? I mean, if she's the kind who likes getting belted — and I agree there are enough of them around — why doesn't she just stay at home, doing what she always did, except now she starts to nag him about not having a job, why not do that? I mean, if she wants to get popped, that would do it."

"I don't know."

"Well, you made a judgment about her character there, Petrolac, let's hear something to back it up. I'm listening. I'm not saying I got her pegged. You tell me."

"Like I said before," Petrolac said, "look how fast she told us to get out of there and you — uh, you . . ."

"I what? Left too fast? Huh? What would you've liked me to do back there — tell her, 'No, no lady, you better let us stick around until your asshole husband does something really stupid'? You think that's the way to do it?"

Petrolac started to speak twice, stopping both times without a word. "Yes — no — aw shit, I don't know."

"Petrolac, listen to me. You paying attention?"

Petrolac nodded. "Yes sir."

"Well remember what I'm telling you now. It is easier to get a nigger speed freak out of a bar — and I don't care what he's holding, knife, razor, pistol — than it is to get between a husband and a wife if you get both of them against you and neither one's got anything more than bare hands. I don't care what color they are or how old.

"You get in a residence and you piss 'em both off, you better get your ass out the door and call for help, 'cause you're going to need it if you try to stay there. And that, my friend, is why that woman didn't have to ask me twice to leave.

"He hadn't done anything to her. He was just rantin' and ravin' at us. And she wasn't gonna sign an information against him for the discolored cheek. And she may not be ready to join the Ladies Auxiliary of the Fraternal Order of Police, but when we left she knew that she had talked to somebody for a while who listened. And the somebody who listened, in psychological shorthand, Petrolac, was a male authority figure — get it? — who listened to what she had to say and didn't punch her out right in the middle of saying it. Now, if she doesn't remember that in any future situation, why hell, she'll be the first. And what that means is, if one of us got to go back, she won't be the one to turn on you. He will. 'Cause he's not in a talking mood. All he wants to do is shout and beat on his chest. Am I getting through to you?"

Petrolac eased the cruiser into Balzic's parking slot beside City Hall. He turned off the engine and said, "Yeah, but, I mean, you're probably right, but I just don't have your experience I guess."

Balzic waited until they were both out of the car before he replied. "Uh, Petrolac, just what the fuck d'you think I been giving you for the last twenty minutes — the benefits of my ignorance? The benefits of my lack of experience? Huh? God-dammit, there are only three ways you get the information — any information. You do it, you talk to somebody who does it, or you read a book by somebody who does it. There may be other ways but I don't know what they are."

"Yes sir."

"Yessir what?"

"Yessir nothing, sir."

"Oh yessir nothing sir my ass. But what?"

"What do you do when two people give you different information?"

"What everybody does, Petrolac. You test it against your own experience and see how it works. And you keep doing whatever works until it doesn't and then you try something else."

"But if I use the wrong way the first time I test it, then what?"

"I already told you. You get your ass out the door and you call for help. Don't ever be ashamed of hollering help. See, Petrolac, it's what I been trying to tell you all night. You got to know when to show your throat. And you got to know that there's no sin in it. Or shame either."

Balzic went up the three concrete stairs into the duty room of the station, feeling suddenly tired, suddenly leaden in his legs.

"I don't know what I'm doing in here," he said, turning around in the duty room and passing Petrolac as he came in. "I'm going home. And tell Stramsky not to bother me."

Balzic, for the second time this day, turned into his own driveway. He was much more clearheaded this time than the last and he somehow regretted the order of his returns and the respective states of his mind. Now's the time I ought to be a little drunk, he thought, walking up the steps and letting himself in.

He had just shut the door and connected the chain lock when he groaned with the memory of what was in store tomorrow.

"Hey, what's the matter with you?" his wife said, walking quickly across the living room toward him.

"I just remembered what happens tomorrow morning."

"What?"

"The union crap. The contract negotiations. Nine o'clock tomorrow in the mayor's office. For a while there tonight I forgot completely about it and boy was that nice."

"Well, keep forgetting about it," Ruth said. "It won't do any

good to think about it now. You want some wine, coffee, a sandwich, what do you want?"

"Oh, don't remind me. Those things caused me more trouble
today than any of 'em were worth."

"What things? What're you talking about?"

"Forget it. Give me a sandwich, give me some wine, skip the
coffee. I'll take a kiss instead."

Ruth canted her head and her eyes took on an impish cast.
"Let me see your teeth."

Balzic threw his arms around her and squeezed. "My teeth are
black from licorice, they're red from pickled beets, they're yellow from ball park mustard, and they're white from milk. I got a
whole rainbow in there. Take your pick. And when you mix 'em
all up, all those colors? You know what they smell like? Huh?
Garlic!"

"Oh you're full of it tonight," she said, feigning an escape
from his breath.

"What're you squirming around for, huh? You don't like my
smell, huh?"

"I like your smell okay. It's that look I'm not sure about."

"What look? Do I got a look?"

"Yeah. It's that old, everybody-get-back-he's-getting-ready-
to-chase-somebody look."

"That one, huh? That's a good look. I like me when I got that
look. But I don't know how come I got it."

"Why not?"

" 'Cause I already caught who I was gonna chase."

"Oh, yeah?"

"Yeeaaah!"

"Mario, you don't pay attention to the calendar," she sang at
him. "I put big X's on the calendar on certain days and you don't
pay attention."

"I don't, huh? Well. I'm gonna start paying attention."

"And when you start paying attention, I'll put another kind
of mark on the calendar, 'cause you know how long you been
saying you would —"

"And I still don't, you mean?"

"And you still don't is exactly what I mean."

"Oh, two years? Ten years? Twenty years?"

"Mario, you look at calendars like a little boy waiting for his birthday, honest to God. You count what you want to count, you don't see anything else. What difference does it make how long you haven't paid attention?"

"Hey, I'm trying. I'm in there pitchin'."

"They are not the same, dearie. Not the same."

"My intentions are honorable though, and my —"

"— heart is pure and you have the strength of ten and you're full of garbanzo beans."

"Awwww, come on."

"Mario, I'm running a flood here! This is my two days to flood. And I don't feel clean when I'm running a flood and you're all the time going 'Awwww.' Quit going 'Awwww' so much and look at the calendar."

"Okay, I'll take a sandwich instead," he said soberly.

"You are so romantic, Mario, you just, boy, you just make me feel so good sometimes. Me or a sandwich." She struggled to pull away and gave him a solid punch in the arm.

"Hey, what's that for?"

"That's for me or a sandwich, that's what that's for. And go brush your teeth. They're still purple."

"Come on, Ruthie, cut me a little slack."

"I'll cut you some bread, you can make your own sandwich, how do you like that, lover boy?"

"Come on then, I love to watch you cut bread. It's the last great erotic experience left for me," he said, reaching down suddenly, catching her in a hug above the knees, and hoisting her over his shoulder and carrying her to the kitchen.

"Mario! Mario! You're nuts. Honest to God, you're crazy. Put me down before you hurt yourself. Whatta you think you are — twenty years old? You'll get a hernia."

Balzic didn't stop until they were by the kitchen sink, and then he eased her off his shoulder so that her bottom came to rest on the counter top.

"Do it, Ruthie. Cut some bread. It really turns me on, honest to God it does. I just see your arm going back and forth like that, the flesh all jiggling and quivery —"

"Mario! What flesh? Jiggling and quivery! Are my arms getting fat?"

Balzic got very close to her and nuzzled her neck and said, "Yeah, but it drives me crazy when you're cuttin' bread."

She pounded on his back with both hands. "Goddamn you," she said, giggling and squealing as he nuzzled her, "you are crazy! It's all that Serbian blood. It got mixed up with that Italian blood and made you crazy!"

They carried on for an hour more, teasing each other, nibbling at cheese and cold ham, and sipping wine until Balzic remembered what he had to do in the morning and how soon morning was going to arrive.

"Shit, I got to go to sleep. You wanna wake me tomorrow?"

"Who's going to if I don't? You haven't heard an alarm clock in twenty years."

"Well, if you were gonna forget one morning, don't make it tomorrow. I'm on nearly everybody's shit list as it is. I show up late, and I'll be on everybody's for sure."

He took one last sip of wine and headed for the bedroom, stripping off clothes as he went. Ruth stayed in the kitchen and washed dishes and put things away, finally folding the dishcloth and hanging it over the faucet, and then she switched on the night lights on the wall and in the stove in case her mother-in-law had to get up during the night. That done, she went into the bedroom and found her husband snoring faintly and still wearing his trousers as he lay on top of the covers.

Rather than struggle with him to get up and take off his trousers and get under the covers, she found a sheet blanket in a chest of drawers and covered him with it. She went to sleep thinking that there had to be a better way to make him pay closer attention to the calendar; what she'd been doing for years now was all the result of foolish optimism, and for all she knew about her husband it would never be anything else. About some things, her husband was a stonehead and this was one of those things. Soon, she thought, soon I'll quit marking that goddamn calendar. She rolled over and sidled close to Mario's ear. "And then you know what's next? Huh? Hot flashes and cold sweats and pennies in my mouth and hammers in my chest. Oh God, mother told me since I was a little girl. Can you hear me?"

He did not.

She rolled away from him. She felt deliciously sleepy and almost as deliciously devilish. Devilment lost. There was no one else awake to play with.

Morning always came too soon for Balzic; on days when he'd drunk too much the night before, it came even sooner. He prepared himself for the day between a series of groans and hurried kisses on the cheeks of his mother, his daughters, and his wife. He was two minutes late for the union negotiations before he ever turned the key in the ignition of his cruiser.

At City Hall he took the stairs two at a time to get to the meeting room on the second floor. For the first time in almost a month, they had begun on time — they being, for the city, Mayor Angelo Bellotti; Councilman Louis Del Vito, chairman of the Safety Committee; and Solicitor Peter Renaldo; and, for the police, Lieutenant Angelo Clemente, who as a desk sergeant had promised everyone he'd retire but who was then promoted and made juvenile officer without Balzic's knowledge or approval; Fraternal Order of Police President Wally Stuchinsky, a state cop; and Joseph Czekaj, FOP solicitor.

For the last week Balzic hadn't been able to stomach any of them. If they hadn't broken up at 4 P.M. every day, Balzic was sure there'd be blood on the table they sat around, and a fine, expensive table it was — nearly sixteen feet long and more than five feet wide and made of highly polished maple that had been varnished but never stained. Mayor Bellotti had smuggled it out of Harrisburg when administrators changed and he'd lost his patronage job in the Department of Property and Supplies. Balzic remembered its arrival clearly: it had been a three-day job for two carpenters and two city laborers to take the table apart, carry it upstairs, and put it together again.

What Mayor Bellotti never told anyone was where he'd stored the table between the time he'd lost his patronage job in Harrisburg and the time he'd got himself elected mayor. Right now, as Balzic slipped into his chair at the far end of the table opposite the mayor but, like the mayor, in between the FOP negotiators on the north side of the table and the city negotiators on the south side, Balzic thought it was probably equally important to know where Mayor Bellotti had stored this monumental piece of furniture in his two years between jobs.

"Would — would somebody make a n-note," Councilman Del Vito said. "The chief of police has arrived." Del Vito was a grocer, with a stutter so bad that if he became trapped on a sound he could hang there for a minute that seemed like an hour and felt like a week. Usually Balzic got along with him very well. It wasn't something Balzic had to work at. Del Vito was a genuinely nice guy and at times startlingly funny — as he was trying to be now by asking somebody to make a note of Balzic's arrival. The joke was that the city was so strapped financially the negotiators had passed the hat, so to speak, to pay for a stenographer from a temporary employment agency. The city council's regular secretary had quit to have a baby and since then everybody connected with the negotiations was bringing in relatives, employees from their private offices, and so on, to maintain records.

For three days they'd had to hire temporary help; yesterday the petty cash had run out at the end of the day and the manager of the employment service wasn't taking city checks.

So Del Vito's crack about somebody making a note of Balzic's arrival should have been funny. It wasn't. Normally, Balzic would have felt something for one of Del Vito's cracks going unappreciated, but right now all he could do was glare at Del Vito and try to figure out where somebody could have stored a table the size of the one they were seated around.

"M-m-make another note," Del Vito said. "The chief of police isn't going to think anything's f-funny today. I can t-t-tell."

Balzic just shook his head and laughed in spite of himself. Nobody else did.

" 'Atta b-boy, Mario," Del Vito said. "At l-least you're on my side today."

"I ain't on anybody's side. I hope I missed everything. I hope you guys settled this goddamn thing. I'm getting sick of looking at everybody in here."

"No such luck, my friend," Mayor Angelo Bellotti said. "We're not even close about the two men in the cars, the overtime, the personal day — what else?"

City Solicitor Pete Renaldo said, "Gentlemen, the arrival of Chief Balzic is duly noted. We are still on the number of officers assigned to patrol cars, could we get on with it?" Renaldo was in his early thirties; his father had been a coal miner and worked all the overtime he could get to make sure his son got through college and law school so he would never have to spend a minute in the mines, and now, Balzic knew, the son despised his father for being a miner, an immigrant, and, worst of all, uneducated. There was no explaining Renaldo's attitude toward his father, but it was well known in Rocksburg and Renaldo did nothing to hide it. Of all the men at the table, Renaldo was the only one with whom Balzic had nothing in common, except one thing: contempt, and it was hard to say who thought less of the other.

"Unless the city," Wally Stuchinsky, FOP president, said after clearing his throat, "unless the city makes some, uh, concedes this a little bit, then we're gonna get stuck on it."

"Mr. Stuchinsky," Renaldo said, "we have been stuck on this issue for two weeks now and for two weeks, morning after morning, you insist on saying the city has to concede this a little bit, is that what you say? 'Concede this a little bit'?"

Stuchinsky nodded. "Yessir, that's what I said and that's what I mean. That's what I mean every time I say it, sir."

Renaldo looked around the room and sighed haughtily. "What happened to the coffee we sent for? Does anyone know?"

Balzic looked at Renaldo and then at Del Vito and then at the mayor. "What's goin' on? We spent three days deciding where everybody was gonna sit. We got that settled and then we spent two days talking about water and coffee and note pads and who was gonna take phone messages and who was gonna talk to the newspaper guys. And now we're back to sending out for coffee again? The goddamn coffee machine is downstairs. And then there's the big coffeepot in the duty room. What's going on, Renaldo?"

"Mr. Renaldo is, uh, not addressing the issues," FOP Solicitor Czekaj said. "Mr. Renaldo is, uh, back to the coffee issue. Which is the non-est nonissue I've ever negotiated." He slumped back in his chair and loosened his tie. Czekaj was a roly-poly man barely five feet five inches tall and when he became disgusted he looked like a fat dwarf with an abscessed tooth. He looked that way now. "Mr. Renaldo is diddling us around again because he can't come up with a reason why two officers shouldn't be assigned to each patrol car in certain areas of the city on certain shifts. This is not an unreasonable item for negotiation. Among reasonable people this would be eminently negotiable. But Mr. Renaldo, I'm sorry to say, has no answer for it and so instead of saying he has no answer for it, he's going to sit here and jerk us all around over where we go to get our goddamn coffee every morning, isn't that right, Mr. Renaldo? I mean, isn't it?"

"If you say so, Mr. Czekaj. The matter of two patrolmen in a car, no matter in what sections of the city or on which shifts of work, is not negotiable because the city simply cannot afford it. That's all there is to it. Hard economic facts. Hard facts. Count the cost, the man-hour cost, and see how the millage rate would go through the roof, and these are the economic facts."

"Bullshit," Czekaj said. "Don't bring that herring into it. We're — you, this council, this mayor is long overdue for a millage increase and they're just playing political football until November and we all know why that is."

Oh shit, Balzic thought, here we go again. Here come the cigars and the wooden matches and Zippos on the union side of the table and the pipes and the butane lighters on the city side and next thing we're going to do is trot out factions of the Democratic Party — without anybody, so help them God, ever saying faction, Democrat, or party. No such words are ever going to cross anybody's lips at this table because this table is full of Democrats. Some of them have even been elected to office.

Czekaj and Stuchinsky could kill Renaldo right now, Balzic thought. They've been on the verge for almost a week. Clemente, old wonderful Clemente who was going to retire until somebody made a him a lieutenant without even telling Balzic, never mind asking whether it was a reasonable idea, Clemente didn't know what the hell was going on. He was just as happy as he could be to be included in something as important as contract negotiations. Old wonderful Lieu-ten-ant Clemente, Balzic thought meanly, could be bought for ten minutes of somebody's sympathy for everything that was wrong with his feet and lower back. Clemente came cheap.

And Stuchinsky and Czekaj knew it, had known it within the first hour of negotiations, and had wondered how in the name of ordinary sense were they supposed to accomplish anything when one of their own could be bought at no cost except a direct, heartfelt gaze into Clemente's eyes as he recounted his physical misery.

Louis Del Vito was nothing if not fair. But every day of his life he heard the economic facts of life from his constituents in his grocery. Whatever the FOP wanted in money wasn't merely to be wished for. There were ladies in felt slippers and not a tooth in their mouths who could read the papers as well as he could, and if he voted raises for the police that weren't right, he would hear it first from mouths full of gums, mouths that talked on this front porch and over that back fence until everybody in Del Vito's wards understood what he had done.

Balzic knew where Renaldo's heart was. It was in a quarry with the other stones.

That left Mayor Angelo Bellotti and himself. As for himself, he knew no cop was paid enough, or got enough days off, or had enough insurance, or had a pension plan that couldn't or wouldn't be raided by two shysters and a computer programmer. The trouble was that everybody around the table knew that Balzic not only served those notions with his mouth but felt them in his bones. His counsel at the table was therefore perceived to be something considerably less than impartial; as such, it was not often sought except privately by Bellotti to see if Balzic couldn't "do something to bring the boys around."

As for Bellotti, well, Balzic thought, old Angelo was a politician. He had grown up running for one office after another, either elected or appointed — sometimes those latter were tougher jobs to win — for as long as Balzic had known him and that was for longer than Balzic wanted to remember. Bellotti knew what every real politician knows. He knew how to bounce, he knew how to fall without breaking anything, he knew how to slip blows to his ego as expertly as any boxer ever slipped blows to his head. Bellotti could be contradicted in mid-sentence by something he himself had said not a week before, and he could not only slip that contradiction and fall against his adversary to catch his breath, but he could bounce back with a smile and a sparkling eye to explain to you how he had not meant anything of the sort. Bellotti may have been kicked out of jobs and voted out of office, but he was never unemployed for long. Nobody could find gainful employment at public expense faster than he could because — and Balzic had to admire him for it — Bellotti was good at what he did and what he did was make people believe it was in their interest to have him for a friend. It was a good thing he had very few appetites. There was no telling what he could steal if he had more.

Balzic mulled all this over and wondered how Czekaj and Stuchinsky were going to get any of what they wanted with one of their own, Clemente, certainly not with them and with Renaldo, Del Vito, and Bellotti wanting to give up nothing against them, each for his own reasons, and with himself as spectator. He had to break something down or they'd be here for another three weeks and the thought of that was beyond comprehending. There'd be blood on this fine table of Bellotti's.

"Listen," Balzic said, interrupting Stuchinsky, who'd been belaboring the issue of assigning a second patrolman to cruisers on certain shifts. "Listen. This is a dead issue. There is no goddamn way we're going to get two people in a patrol car and I don't care what shift you're talking about."

"Mario!" Stuchinsky cried out.

"No, no, just listen a minute. You guys have been going round and round on this and I've kept my mouth shut, but no more. You're playing games here and I'm sick of it. Do what you want on the rest, but this issue is numbers plain and simple. Unless somebody dies — 'cause nobody I know is gonna retire in the next two years — nobody is gonna authorize the hiring of even one more man. The force stays the same. We just got two new black-and-whites, the two four-wheelers were new last year, and my cruiser's only two years old. So that number's not gonna change. Now if those two numbers are not gonna change, then all this yimmer-yammer about two guys in a car is bullshit.

"Now bullshit's fine if it only lasts a couple of days until everybody finds out where everybody's gonna sit and so on, but this thing's been going on for damn near two weeks. Every day it comes up, and I know the hustle. You give us this, we won't ask for that, we get this, we won't give you that, and whatever. But for crissake, get off this one dead horse, will you? This horse's not only dead, he's been laying out in the sun, he's all puffed up and getting ready to split and throw stink on everybody."

"Mario," Stuchinsky said, when he could get his mouth together to start talking, "what the hell — why are — hell, you know better'n anybody here a guy out on his own, he can be in a jackpot that fast!" Stuchinsky snapped his fingers. "We been talking this issue for weeks now and just — I just think the other side here was gonna come around —"

"Concede a little?" Renaldo said, smiling genuinely at the table for the first time Balzic could remember. "I told you, Mr. Stuchinsky, this was a matter of hard economic fact —"

"Oh shut the hell up, Renaldo," Balzic said.

"I beg your pardon!"

"You heard me. Shut the hell up! Stuchinsky is sitting there thinking I've thrown a screw into him and you're sitting there gloating. Knock it off.

"Hard, economic facts, my ass. The facts are simple arith-metic. No more police, no more vehicles. Those numbers stay the same. We can all sit here and say yeah, damn right, nobody should be out there on his own, but that's what the hell we got radios for. And if you're gonna want two men in a vehicle, the next thing you'll want is two men on a beat and then two men with dogs and then two men at every intersection during rush hour traffic. Now that's silly. And we all know it's silly, so let's forget about it, 'cause we got as much chance of putting two men in every intersection at rush hours as we got of getting two men in each vehicle.

"Stuchinsky — Wally — I'm on your side, but you're wasting breath on this one. We'll continue to work as we have for the last ten or fifteen years, ever since we went to five vehicles. The man gets in a jackpot — doesn't matter whether he's on his ass in a warm car in the winter or on his feet in a thunderstorm — he calls for help. I got rid of all the heroes on this force. Long ago. They never got past probation."

"Mario, I couldn't've said it better myself —"

"Oh Angelo, for crissake."

"No, Mario, I mean it," Mayor Bellotti said. "There's just one thing. I'm glad you brought up about the radios, uh, we been getting mail from Washington, uh, from the FCC, you know, the communications people, and they've been receiving com-plaints about the profanity that's being used on our channels."

"What?"

"That's right, Mario, that's what they say. They say between you and the fire chief, the air is, uh, to say the least, a little blue."

"Oh, Angelo, come on. Christ. What is it now, all the people with their little home monitors, their little hundred-dollar police scanners, huh? We change the frequency every three months as it is. The firemen aren't going to change their frequency. They're volunteers. They all got the same cheap equipment that's trying to pick us up. If the FCC has a bitch with the fire chief that's not my problem —"

"But, Mario, there is a very heavy fine for using profanity on the air like you're doing."

"Oh bullshit. Who made the complaints? Some goody-two-shoes Presbyterian who's afraid to walk a block from where he lives so he looks at the tube and tries to listen to us. He thinks that shit he sees on the tube is what's happening outside his house and then because those cops on TV don't swear he thinks we're not supposed to. Well fuck him and all the rest of 'em. Tell 'em to come look at me when they say they don't like my words. I ain't television. Tell 'em to get off my fuckin' channel. And what the hell's Washington doing — they don't have anything better to do but listen to shit complaints like that? No wonder the fuckin' communists are winning all over the world."

"That's a wonderful speech, Mr. Balzic," Renaldo said. "Maybe you'd care to deliver it to the PTA or to some rosary altar societies I can think of."

Balzic sighed and said under his breath, "I hope you get hit by a bus, you cackaroach."

"Me, I liked your speech, M-Mario," Del Vito said. "A little h-hammy, but effective. Y-you can come down my store and we'll sell t-tickets. We should get, oh, th-three or f-four people at least. You'll be a sen-sensation."

"Could we please get on with it?" Czekaj said, scowling through the smoke of his cigar. "This is all informative and warm and so on and so forth, but could we please get on with it? Hmm?"

"Good idea," Balzic said. "You guys get on with it. I'm going downstairs to see what's going on in my department."

"Somebody make a n-note. The police chief lasted almost until the f-first coffee b-break."

"I'm gonna come down to your store," Balzic said. "I'm gonna order a hundred hoagies and then I'm not gonna pick 'em up."

"That's already been t-tried. Anything over five is s-strictly c-cash. What do I look like? A c-cop?"

"Could we please get on with it?" Czekaj said again. "You guys want to work up a comedy routine, do it on your own time. I'm costing the FOP fifty bucks an hour. And that's my sale price."

Clemente thought that was the funniest thing he'd heard yet.

He laughed so hard tears came to his cheeks and mucus to his upper lip.

Balzic knew for sure it was time to go downstairs. Without a word, he did.

He could still hear Clemente snorting his laughter when he was starting down the stairs. Why was he so mad at Clemente, he wondered. He once almost loved Clemente like a brother. He certainly respected him as a cop. And why should he resent Clemente's promotion? Worse, why should he keep on resenting it? It wasn't Clemente's fault that the promotion had been offered to him. So what if he didn't understand that he'd been thrown a bone. At Clemente's age and in his condition, sometimes bones were all there were. So what if he didn't comprehend that he got the promotion because he was most likely to be named one of the FOP's negotiators for this contract.

Balzic gave all the slack he could to Clemente, but he still couldn't quit being angry. And he knew why and that made it even worse. Clemente's health had gone. He had indeed had much trouble with his feet. All the old stale jokes about a policeman's feet pertained to Clemente, and then some. In addition to all the usual complaints — fodder fit for cartoons despite their reality — Clemente also had stress fractures in his shinbones and all of those problems had thrown his spine out of alignment. Clemente wasn't even fifty. He looked sixty-five and at times he acted ninety.

Balzic had seen a friend's health go bad over the stuff of cartoons and had seen him age gracelessly and had lost respect for him. And it was not Clemente's fault that he tried to better himself and took the promotion and the raise and went back on his word of only several months ago that he would retire.

Balzic was feeling small and mean and guilty and spiteful. And there was only himself to aim those emotions at. If he didn't start thinking about something or someone else he was going to be awfully bad company for himself.

He strode into the duty room and found Patrolman Harry Lynch at the radio console. Lynch was scowling and drumming his fingers on the arms of the chair.

Since Clemente's promotion to lieutenant, several patrolmen with time in grade and high scores on the sergeant's test were rotating into the seven-to-three watch as desk sergeant. Lynch had been at it for less than a week and he loathed it. Lynch was six feet four and a solid two hundred pounds. When a drunk was causing a commotion somewhere, anybody who was on duty and in the area answered the call. When somebody got out of hand in the black joints, the call came in and Lynch was asked for by the complainant. No other beat officer on the force could make that claim — or wanted to.

"You gotta get me the hell outta here, Mario," Lynch said. His finger-drumming grew louder as Balzic approached.

"Hey, Harry, if you didn't want the stripes, why'd you take the test?"

"Mario, everybody takes the goddamn test. It's what you do. It's expected. Your family expects it, you expect it, and I expect it. When you get your time in, you take the fucking test. How was I supposed to know I was gonna do so good on it?"

"You wanna take the test over so you can fuck it up?"

"Come on, Mario, you know what I mean."

"No. I don't. What do you mean? You don't want the job? Just say so and I'll make sure you don't get it. I'll tell the safety committee you made a pass at me."

"Not that fuckin' way," Lynch bellowed, half rising out of the chair.

Balzic turned away to look for a coffee cup. "Relax, Harry. You won't get the job. Your sense of humor ain't what it used to be. And if you're gonna put up with the shit that goes on at that desk you gotta be able to laugh or you wind up like Clemente, looking for sympathy everywhere and making guys like me hate myself."

"Well you don't joke about shit like that, Mario. I don't want to lose the job I got. I just don't want this one, and that ain't funny, what you said."

"At ease, Harry, at ease. I take it all back, okay?" Balzic found a clean cup and filled it with coffee and then headed for his own office at the far end of the room. He stepped inside and then stuck his head back out and yelled to Lynch, "I take it back, Harry, okay? I won't tell 'em you made a pass at me, okay? I'll tell 'em I saw you making a pass at Clemente."

Balzic shut the door and locked it as Lynch came bellowing out of the chair.

"Goddamnit, Mario, that ain't funny. Anybody happened to hear that and didn't understand or nothing and that could've caused me a lot of embarrassment and explaining. I mean, I knew you were joking even if it wasn't funny, but —"

"I know, Harry, that's why I locked myself in here. So you could have enough time to remember that I was joking."

There was no reply.

"Can I come back out now, Harry?"

"Hey, you're the chief."

"That's not what I asked you. We both know that. I want to know if I can come back out."

"Yeah. I ain't mad anymore."

Balzic unlocked the door and stuck his head out, grinning half maliciously, half apologetically. "Is it okay? No shit?'"

"Aw come on, Mario. Sometimes you make me out to be some kind of fuckin' animal."

Balzic stepped out of his office and had to turn his face away for a moment in order not to show Lynch how much he wanted to respond to that one.

"I don't care, Mario, just as long as nobody else hears, 'cause they wouldn't understand. But sometimes you go a little too far, you know?"

"Come on, Harry. I been upstairs listening to all the smoke getting pumped up everybody's ass up there, if I can't come down here and joke around a little bit, I mean, what the hell. You know I'd never say anything like that in front of somebody and you know I'm just pulling your chain a little bit. Come on, cut me a little slack."

"Hey, it's cut, it's cut," Lynch walked back toward the radio and slumped his long, muscular frame into the chair. "But I'm not joking about not wanting this job. Shit, I'd go crazy. You know what the first call I got this morning was, huh? Some woman wanted her paperboy arrested. Two days now he didn't put the paper where he usually puts it. I mean, she was seriously pissed.

"And the next call I got was from some guy who wanted me to come and tell the gas company to quit tearing up the street in front of his house. He couldn't sleep because of the air hammer. And he was seriously pissed also. That's the way my day started and, I'll tell you, I don't wanna make a career out of this, nossir, I don't. And I ain't either."

"You convinced me," Balzic said. "I'm sold. Don't waste another minute worrying about it. Just do out your week and forget it."

The phone rang then and Lynch warily picked up the headset and put it on.

"Rocksburg Police, Lynch speaking . . . yes ma'am . . . yes ma'am, I do too remember you . . . He still didn't come home yet . . . Well the chief's right here if you want to talk to him . . . yes ma'am, here he is." Lynch looked at Balzic and said, "Where you wanna take it, here or in your office?"

"Transfer it onto my line. I wouldn't want you to not be able to answer the phone." Balzic stepped quickly into his office, pushed the lighted button on his phone, picked up the receiver, and identified himself.

"This is Frances Romanelli and —"

"And you still have your problem."

"Yes."

"Only what?"

"I don't know only what," she said. "Last night after you left, Jimmy stayed here for a little while, and then he said he was going out to get a six-pack of beer."

"And he didn't come back."

"Yes. No, he didn't come back."

"Mrs. Romanelli, uh, Frances, where'd your husband say he got that money last night?"

"You heard that? I thought Jimmy was just acting paranoid again."

"No, I was eavesdropping. I heard him say something about a thousand bucks. Where'd he say he got it?"

"Playing cards."

"Where'd he say he was playing cards?"

"At one of his friend's house. It's a guy he used to hunt with."

"He ever play cards there before?"

"Oh sure. Lots of times. There were six or seven guys, they'd all rotate. We used to have the game here every six or seven weeks."

"Uh-huh. And what were the stakes?"

"The stakes?"

"Yeah, you know. How much did they play for?"

"Oh, it was nickels and dimes for one kind of game and then I think they'd play for quarters and halves when they played another kind of game."

"Did Jimmy ever win anything like a thousand dollars before?"

"Are you kiddin'? He never won a hundred. He never won thirty. Come to think of it he never even lost more than ten or fifteen dollars either."

"Did anybody else?"

"I don't know. I was never allowed to play in those games. I was only allowed to play for pennies when Jimmy's sisters and their husbands came over. I wasn't allowed in the big games."

"In the big games?"

"Well that's what Jimmy called them."

"Were you allowed in the same room?"

"Well of course I was. How else was I going to serve the sandwiches . . . oh, that was a joke, wasn't it?"

"Uh, maybe not a very good joke." Balzic sipped some coffee. "Frances, is there, uh, is there something you want me to do about Jimmy? Today I mean?"

"I don't know. I really don't. He's acting so crazy lately. Sometimes he's so hyped up and other times, other times it's like he's in a fog."

"Was he hyped up last night — is that what you'd call hyped up, the way he was last night?"

"Definitely, that's exactly what I mean. But other times he's like — drunk. Except he isn't drunk. He doesn't smell from beer. And beer is all he drinks. He can't stand vodka. Isn't that the one you're not supposed to be able to smell on somebody if they been drinking it?"

"That's what they say. Well, look, Frances, you want me to do something? You want me to get people looking for him, huh?"

"Yeah. Sure. That's why I called."

"Okay. Okay. I'll do it. And I'll have somebody check back with you every four hours or so. Now where you gonna be?"

"I'm going to be right here. I called off sick on both my jobs. And I'm not going to school today. At the community college, you know?"

"I know. Uh, one more thing. Did he go where — I mean, did he say he was going to get beer last night where he usually gets it?"

"No. He didn't say. But he only goes one place. That's down the end of the street. At Ripulsky's."

"Okay, we'll start there. Don't worry, we'll turn something up."

Balzic hung up and then turned the wheel file on his desk looking for a phone number. He found the one he was looking for and dialed it.

"State Bureau of Drug Enforcement, Russell speaking."

"Russell my ass. Russellini you mean."

"Who is this?"

"Who else knows your real name besides you and your parents, you dumb dago."

"Is this you, Balzic? Hey, what're you doing? You still chief of police of that dump? When you gonna get a good job? I'll bet your mother cries every night, waiting for you to get a decent job."

"Hey, Russellini Russell, I got a good job. If my mother cries, she cries for you. She wants to know if you got baptized all over again or was it all paperwork? Did you get your hair wet? Or did it just cost you money to change your name? That's what she cries about."

"Yeah, yeah, yeah. So whatta you want, now that you made your point, Small Time Chief, huh?"

"I want to know if the name Romanelli means anything to you."

"Yeah, we got a Romanelli on our active sheet. Why?"

"What's his first name and where's he live?"

"Um, that would be James. Jimmy the coal miner. He lives, uh, your way, one of the little townships around you. Kennedy, it seems to me sounds right."

"You looking this up or you got it in your head?"

"In my head."

"Is he that active, huh, that you got him on the top of your head?"

"Nah, he's not active active. We figure him for a stasher. But nothing's moved in any quantity worth breaking down his door and tearing his house and car apart, if you know what I mean."

"How long's he been this way?"

"Um, I think we started following him like six, seven months ago. You know, we didn't go out of our way, understand, but when we didn't have anything else to do, one of us'd peel off and stay with him a while. He throws an awful lot of twenties around for a guy who hasn't worked in over a year."

"But he doesn't move anything?"

"Nah, he's definitely not a mover and shaker. He's too dumb. Always travels the same roads, the same speed, never pays any attention to who's behind him. With that attitude, he's not moving anything."

"So how do you know?"

"Hey, Mario, he hangs out in the right places with the right people, and he's always got a handful of twenties. You can't afford the way he lives on unemployment checks. But as I said before, we're not really watching him — at least not yet. Now his friends, they're a different story. They're very big in rented trucks. Big trucks. Know what I mean? They like those big trucks. I'd like to have the money they pay the rental companies.

And the way they take care of those trucks! So clean, you wouldn't believe it. You could eat in those trucks, when they bring 'em back. Very clean fellas. They're moving a lot of merchandise, but we don't know where they put it. Those fuckers, they pay attention to who's behind them. And they know the roads of this county like nobody in this office knows 'em. Am I answering your question?"

"Yeah, better than I expected. These guys got a clubhouse?"

"Mostly they stay on the roads. But they go to Pittsburgh a lot and then they go to a place up the road from you, a spaghetti house, that one with no name, the one that just says 'Spaghetti' in neon, you know the one I mean?"

"Yeah, on the road to Bovard Township."

"That's the one. Very clubby in there, very fraternal with the owner. But he's squeaky clean, that guy. We run him through all the computers, the only bad time he ever did was KP in the army in World War II. Name's Tripoli. Girardo Tripoli. Gerry the spaghetti man. You know him?"

"I know who he is. He makes great sauce. Or at least he used to. I haven't been in his place for years. I don't know why I quit going. Anything else you can tell me about Romanelli?"

"Nah. That's all I know. I figure him for a money stasher, maybe heat, but definitely nothing else. Most likely money."

"Okay, my friend. Say hello to your family."

"You too."

Balzic hung up and wondered how deeply Jimmy Romanelli was in. If he was stashing money for dealers, the fee was usually ten percent. A thousand bucks as a percentage meant that he wasn't very trusted or the people who were giving him the money to stash were not as big as Officer Russell of the state Bureau of Drug Enforcement thought they were. But since Russell had described Romanelli's friends as being very interested in big rental trucks, it was more likely that his friends were testing Romanelli with only so much to stash. That was normal, and much more plausible. Now. How much of this news should Mrs. Romanelli know? How much did she know? How much information did she have to fill in gaps?

Oh well, worry about that later, Balzic thought, reaching for the Rocksburg phone directory and looking for the number for Ripulsky's bar or tavern or saloon or grille or whatever it was called.

It was called simply "Ripulsky's." Thatta boy, Balzic thought, dialing the number, keep it simple.

"Hello."

"Ripulsky's?"

"Yeah."

"This is Mario Balzic, chief of police in Rocksburg. I'd like to talk to whoever was tending bar last night."

"You got him."

"And who are you?"

"Who the hell you think? Ripulsky. Who else? You think I got bartenders? Ha."

"Okay. Mr. Ripulsky, you know a James Romanelli? Jimmy Romanelli?"

"Yeah. I know him."

"Was he in your place last night?"

"Nope."

"Think about it, Mr. Ripulsky, this is important."

"I don't care how important it is. I don't have to think about it. He wasn't here last night."

"You sound very sure of yourself."

"Hey, you asked me a question, I give you the answer. You gonna argue with me now?"

"No, I'm not. I just want to know how you can be so sure, that's all."

"You never been in my place, huh?"

"No, I haven't," Balzic said.

"It ain't the ballroom at the Pittsburgh Hilton. I got six stools, two tables, a seven-foot pool table, a pinball, and a TV. I get twelve people in here, I don't have a crowd — I got New Year's Eve, you know? Besides which, I ain't seen a new face in here in over a year, that's how long it's been since a new face moved into the patch."

"Okay. So there's no doubt Romanelli wasn't there last night?"

"No doubt. He was here the day before. He brung me some tomatoes. Pretty expensive tomatoes."

"Oh? Why's that?"

"I made him a bet. He said he could grow tomatoes in June. I told him he was full of you know what and I bet him. Those tomatoes cost me a few bucks."

"So you know him then."

"Sure. He's lived in that house all his life. I bought this place a year before he was born. I'm in here forty-two years next January."

"You know him pretty good?"

"Good enough."

"You notice any change in him lately?"

"Yeah. He ain't working. That's a big change in any man's life. You're working, bringing home the change, the world ain't so bad. You ain't working, you're bringing home what the state gives you, and then that runs out, the world ain't worth cold piss."

"And that's the only change you noticed in him, huh?"

"Nah, that wasn't no change in him. It just made him worse. He always been a bitcher. He don't like this, he don't like that, and nobody knows anything but him. It ain't his fault. His old man was a rotten bastard. Nothing Jimmy did could make the old man happy. He was always yelling at the kid, smacking him around, smacking his old lady around. He was a prick, that's all. A prick's a prick."

"So Jimmy hasn't really changed. I mean, being out of work just exaggerated what he is, right, is that what you're saying?"

"That's it."

"Well, Mr. Ripulsky, I don't want to wear you out, I'm sure you got work to do —"

"You kiddin'? I ain't had nobody in here for over an hour. How many times can you wash the glasses?"

"Well, then, okay, if you got some time, uh, have you noticed that Romanelli seems to have any more money than he usually had?"

"Money? He's on unemployment — no, he's done with that.

He's living on his wife. Wait a minute. Come to think of it, I did see him with money a couple of times and he said he won it playing poker. Well, that was baloney 'cause we used to play in here sometimes and he's a lousy poker player. He calls everything. Nobody could bluff when he was playing. He always said he couldn't be bluffed — you know anything about poker?"

"Enough."

"Yeah, so that's what I mean. Guys like that, they get killed. But it was a big thing with him. 'You ain't gonna bluff me,' he used to always say. So I don't know where he's getting this money. But I know it really busts his balls to live off his old lady. And she's such a nice little girl. But he's a fuckin' hardhead. Though, like I say, it ain't really his fault, you know, so I guess I know how to get along with him is what I'm trying to tell you. He really don't have no friends.

"He had a bunch of guys he thinks are his friends, but they was just using him."

"How'd they do that?" Balzic said.

"Aw, well, he had this cabin up on the reservoir and he always had a lot of guns and a boat and fishing rods and stuff like that there, and these guys was always using his stuff. And he didn't have nothing but the best. Most of the guys around here, they buy their huntin' guns in the discount stores, not him. He got shotguns from Italy and Spain and Japan and paid top dollar for 'em.

"And his friends, they'd borrow 'em and borrow 'em and pretty soon they'd have his stuff more than he would. And then he'd start bitchin' and moanin' and cryin' the blues. 'Everybody's no fuckin' good' and this and that and he'd wear your ears out about the people he did all this stuff for and they were just using him — and they were — but then they'd come around and it'd start all over. I told him one time, I said, 'Jimmy, trouble with you is you don't know nothing about friends.' And he don't. It's almost like, well, like, uh . . ."

"Like what?" Balzic said.

"Like, uh, he gotta get himself in a position where people

screw him just so he can keep on saying that people'll screw you, you know?"

"I'm beginning to understand," Balzic said. "Well listen, Mr. Ripulsky, you've been a lot of help, really."

"Well ain't you gonna tell me what all this was about?"

"No, I don't think so. But if he comes in there, you tell him to call me or call home, 'cause his wife is worried, whether he believes it or not. Does that tell you anything?"

"Tells me enough. Okay. I'll tell him if I see him. Listen, you stop out some time, buy ya a beer, shoot the stuff. You don't sound like the usual pain-in-the-ass cop to me."

"Did somebody say I was?"

"No, but most cops are, you know? At least the ones I know. They're either saying, 'Lemme see your license,' or else they got their hands out."

"Well, I don't wanna see your license and if I ever do stop around, Mr. Ripulsky, I'll buy *you* one, okay?"

"Okay."

Balzic said good-bye and hung up.

Lynch stuck his head in the door and said, "Uh, they want you upstairs. The mayor came down while you were on the phone. I told him I'd tell you."

Balzic nodded and said, "Well, I ain't going upstairs. I don't know where I'm going but I do know it ain't upstairs. I listened to all that shit I'm gonna listen to."

"What am I supposed to tell them?"

"Tell them you told me like you were supposed to. After that it's not your problem, right?"

"I guess," Lynch said, shaking his head as though what went on in this office was the most incomprehensible thing in the world. "I'll sure be glad when this fuckin' week's over."

"Relax, Harry. It's not that tough. All you got to understand around here is that most people want to mean something to somebody else and as long as you know that you can always come up with an answer — no matter what the question is."

"Well, uh, just where you gonna be if they don't want to take what you say I should say for an answer?"

"Tell them whatever you want, Harry. I got something bothering me and I don't know where I'm going or how long I'm gonna be. The only thing for sure I know is I'm not going upstairs to listen to those guys pump smoke up each other's ass, okay?"

"You're the chief."

"That's right, Harry, and you're a beat patrolman trying to learn how to be a desk sergeant. On-the-job training. You're doing it yourself. Nobody helping you. They come down and ask you where I am, that's what you tell them. And you tell them if Clemente hadn't gotten promoted to lieutenant you wouldn't be in the spot you're in. How's that, Harry? Does that sound pretty good?"

"I can't say nothing about Clemente. He's just looking out for himself."

"I'm not talking about Clemente, Harry. I'm talking about the double-breasted bastards that gave him that promotion so he'd wind up sitting where he's sitting now."

"I don't know nothin' about that," Lynch said, shaking his head as though he truly did not know anything about it.

"Sure you don't. You're as dumb as everybody thinks you are."

"What's that supposed to mean?" Lynch said, stiffening in the doorway.

"Nothing, Harry, forget it. Just know this, okay? The mayor and a couple of his friends, including the City Solicitor Renaldo, really put a job on me and Lou Del Vito. They promoted Clemente without telling me — and I'm supposed to be the chief — or Del Vito — and he's supposed to be the chairman of the safety committee. They caught us looking the other way. We go to Pittsburgh to hear some guy from Washington give a speech and when we come back we find out they called a special meeting to promote what's-his-face upstairs.

"Now when push comes to shove up there, just whose side do you think Clemente's gonna be on? Huh? I mean, after he thinks about the raise and the retirement and the cruiser he gets all for himself and the plain clothes and the speeches he's gonna make to the Parent-Teachers — just what d'you think is gonna be going through his head when he looks across the table and sees the two guys who got him all that, huh?

"I'll tell you what's gonna happen, Harry. The guys he's supposed to be working with, Stuchinsky and Czekaj, they're gonna get pissed. And when they finally see what they're up against — I mean they know it already — but when they discover it's even worse than they suspected, they're gonna do what anybody would do. They're gonna tuck their chins down and bull their necks and get what's called in negotiations, uh, intransigent."

"What the hell's that?"

"You know how a guy gets when he's drunk and he's in a corner and you say to him, 'Hey, you may as well put the knife down 'cause I can wait just as long as you can,' and he looks at you and he says, 'The fuck you can.' You know how that little scene goes, Harry?"

"Yeah," Harry said quickly, because that little scene was one he did understand.

"Well, when that guy gives you his 'The fuck you can,' that's intransigence, Harry. And that's what Stuchinsky and Czekaj are gonna do. And you know what that means?"

"No, what?"

"That means you guys are gonna strike. And that means that instead of me spending ten or twelve hours a day down here, I'll be moving in for the duration. And nobody where I live — including me — is in love with that thought. Which is a long way around to tell you, Harry, that I don't give a shit what you tell anybody from upstairs who comes looking for me. I'm taking a hike out of here. See you later."

Balzic walked quickly past a perplexed and scowling Lynch.

He had no idea where he was going; all he knew was that he was going. Sometimes it was better to run from something than toward something even if you had to say the reverse to keep people from looking at you funny. Usually at times like this he would drive out to the Police Rod and Gun Club rifle and pistol range and take out his Springfield 30.06 and lose himself in the squeezing off of shots at paper targets. He'd been doing that less and less of late, not that he didn't drive out to the range and take the rifle out of his trunk and monkey with the scope and just fiddle with it generally. But less and less did he feel the need for putting live rounds in the chamber and squeezing them off until the explosion took him by surprise. Now he felt content to dry-fire the rifle, to practice breathing and squeezing off the shot with no cartridge to explode, no recoil, no smell of powder. All there was was a snap of the firing pin in the bolt and Balzic's intuition that his breathing and squeezing had been right and had produced a hit or had been wrong and had produced something less. If it did nothing else, dry-firing saved on ammunition and it saved cleaning the rifle. When dry-firing was doing what he intended it to do, it gave him a calmness and peace he could not explain — the several times that he'd tried to explain it he'd felt like a fool — and yet he knew it was no less real for his being unable to speak about it coherently.

Lately, sometimes it was enough for him merely to open the trunk and look at the rifle and to imagine himself holding it and breathing and squeezing the trigger and then cocking the bolt and breathing and squeezing again. Either I'm getting wiser, he thought, or else I'm heading down the big slide to senile psychosis.

So it was that halfway to the Rod and Gun Club range, he stopped suddenly, did a U turn in three swings of the car on the narrow macadam, and drove out to Kennedy Township. He had no idea where he was going. There were only three places there that he either logically or sensibly could have gone: he could have gone to Jimmy Romanelli's house to see how Frances was doing and if Jimmy had come back; or he could have gone to see old man Fiori to renew a friendship; or he could have gone where he was going, past both those houses to the end of the street to Ripulsky's.

"I think I popped the cork," Balzic said aloud to himself. "Just what in the hell am I doing here? Am I hiding out? What the hell am I doing?"

He got out of the car and stood looking at Ripulsky's, dis-

tinguishable from all the other houses of the patch only by two
signs hanging above the door. One was a metal sign that said
"Ripulsky's" in red letters on a white background and under-
neath it hung a yellow electric sign that said in black letters,
simply, "Beer."

Balzic walked to the door, opened it, and was greeted by
hoots of laughter. The bar, looking pretty much as Balzic believed it would from Ripulsky's description — twelve people
would have indeed been a New Year's party — was deserted,
save for the one person who was hooting and shrieking with
laughter from behind the bar.

Balzic stepped to the bar and had to lean over to see the person
behind it, a woman of great age, bent nearly double, her hair
yellow-gray, her skin speckled and parched, her mouth tooth-
less, her eyes clouded over with the beginning milkiness of
cataracts, and all bundled to the neck in a bulky wool sweater
though the temperature outside was near eighty and not much
cooler where she was.

"Hello goo-bye. Vine, visky, beer? Vat you like? Huh? Go
home! No drink. Kiss vife. Push-push," she said, straightening
herself so that she was bent only at a thirty-degree angle from
the hips up instead of what seemed to have been a forty-five-
degree bend before.

"I'll have a beer," Balzic said.

"Ten dollar."

"God, I only want one," Balzic said, laughing.

"Ten dollar," she said again, hooting afterward.

"Just one beer. Any kind. I'll give you fifty cents for it."

"Hokay. Big sale today. Fifty cents. Then go home. Get ta
hell out. Kiss vife, kids. Go picnic. No drink." She toddled off,
her tongue clicking against the roof of her mouth amid squeals
of laughter. She descended on a beer cooler and, in movements so
slow Balzic had the feeling something was altering time, she
reached down and brought up a bottle of beer. She returned and
put it on the bar in front of him without opening it.

"You going to open it?" Balzic said.

"Fifty cents for beer."

"Okay," Balzic said, producing two quarters, which the woman picked up as slowly as she'd gotten the beer.

"You going to open it now?"

She shook her head slowly, emphatically, from side to side.

"Why not?"

"Beer fifty cents. Vant open, nine dollar fifty cent."

Balzic smiled in spite of himself. "Lady, I don't know whether you know what your hustle is, but I do and I ain't going for it."

"Ya, ya. Go home. Don't drink. Kiss vife, take kids picnic."

Balzic leaned on the bar and shook his head. Helluva job of running away I did, he thought.

"Hey, Missus, you got an opener? Huh? Yoo-hoo, hey, missus. You wanna open my beer?"

She had eased herself onto a wooden kitchen chair, her knees far apart, her hands folded and quaking slightly in the hammock of her skirt formed by her splayed knees.

"Go home. No drink. No open. Kiss vife, no stay. Get to hell out, ya?" She began to rock back and forth.

Balzic heard footsteps and then a curtain being pulled aside and he looked beyond the woman to see a man rubbing sleep out of his eyes. He was short but very wide and his stomach showed a love of food and drink. His left arm stopped just above where the elbow should have been.

"Okay, Momma, I can take over now," he said to the old woman.

"No, no, go sleep back. Only him." She pointed with her chin at Balzic. "He no drink. No open. Tell him get ta hell out, ya? But stay. You go sleep back, no vorry. I look."

"That's all right, Momma. I can take over now. Go on, back, lay down, watch television."

"Ou, ou, Cheesou Chrees, I go, I goin'. Make pay him. Nine fifty dollar make pay him. Then open, kay?"

"Okay, Momma, don't worry. I'll get him, I'll make him pay." He helped the woman to her feet and guided her back the same route he had come. After a minute's conversation — audible to Balzic only as a murmur — the man returned. He walked unhurriedly to Balzic, took the bottle of beer, opened it, and returned it to the bar. He then reached behind him to the back bar for a glass and put that beside the bottle.

"Uh, your mother's quite a woman," Balzic said, pouring beer into the glass.

"Be careful what you say, my friend," the man said. "I only got a couple rules in here. No fuckin', no fightin', no credit, and no cracks about my mother."

"Mr. Ripulsky, I wouldn't say anything unkind about your mother. I have a mother myself. I feel exactly the same way."

"Then we understand one another," Ripulsky said nodding. "You know me, but I never saw you before."

"We talked on the phone a little while ago. I'm Balzic."

"Oh, yeah, yeah, the cop. Hey, you took me up pretty fast on the drink."

"No, no. I'll pay. I just wanted to come out and talk a little bit."

"About what? Romanelli. Huh?"

"Oh, him maybe. I don't know. Just a little conversation, see how the patch is doing, you know."

"Well, for guys who wanna work, the patch is still okay. Fourteen months ago, now, that was a different story. Everybody was pissin' and moanin' and cryin' in their beer, you know. The mine closes over in Westfield Township, that was a blow. A real blow. But like I said, the guys who wanna work, they found jobs. They're digging coal. Other guys, well, you know, they run the checks right out to the end and then they go get something."

"Guys like Romanelli," Balzic said, "what do they do?"

"No, it's not 'guys' like him. Not around here. It's just him. Everybody else who got shit on when that mine went out, even if they played their unemployment checks right out to the end, they still found a job somewhere. Some of 'em had to move to Ohio, some of 'em went to West Virginia, but they all got something. Nah," Ripulsky said, shaking his head, "not Jimmy, Jimmy's a goddamn baby. Nice guy, you understand, as long as

everything's goin' his way. Then he's everybody's pal. But it
don't go his way, then you got to get some diapers for him,
otherwise he'll start making messes everywhere."

Ripulsky paused and cocked his head and looked, squinty and
puckered, squarely into Balzic's eyes. "You gonna tell me what
this is about? Huh? Before I say something stupid?"

"Mr. Ripulsky, I'll bet you haven't said anything stupid in so
long you can't remember it."

"Oh! Ha! I say something stupid every day. But no kiddin'
now, what's all this about Romanelli?"

"Well, see, a long time ago . . ." Balzic began, and recounted
for Ripulsky how Mr. Fiori and Balzic's father were friends and
how he, Balzic, had watched Fiori's daughter, Frances, now Mrs.
Romanelli, while the men talked and drank wine and ate peppers
in the sun under the grape arbor.

"Ah, so you got kinda a special regard for the family, huh?"
Ripulsky said, nodding. "Yeah, well, I can see how you'd like to
stop something before it got started — is that what you're trying
to do?"

"Something like that."

"Well, speaking for myself," Ripulsky said, "Jimmy's a dis-
appointment to me. I always tried to, uh, well, knowing how his
father was, I always went out of my way to show him that not
all adults were pricks like his old man, you know?"

"I know," Balzic said.

"But when things don't go good for him, I swear to God, he
acts just like his old man did. Pigheaded, stubborn, Jesus,
couldn't tell him nothing. And ever since the mine closed,
Jimmy's been just like that. He don't wanna know nothin' about
how to do some good for himself. It's all everybody's fault but
his and that's that." Ripulsky shook his head. "Why do people
gotta act like that? Huh? Course, you gotta deal with people like
that every day, huh? I wouldn't want your job for nothing.
Course, I couldn't do it neither." He nodded toward the stump
of his left arm.

"What happened?" Balzic said.

"Oh, some Germans didn't like me coming ashore in France.

I was in World War II five seconds. The front of the boat
dropped, I hit the water, no shit, my left foot, I step in the water,
and the next thing I know I'm on a ship going back to England,
bandages all over my arm and head and bottles hanging all
around, and that was it. World War II. Pffft! Five seconds. Left
foot in the water, never got on land, I still don't know what hit
me. I never saw another guy who was in my platoon. I don't
know what happened to 'em. And, uh, I hung around in England, they operated on me there, and then they shipped me back
here. To Atlantic City, one of those big hotels on the boardwalk,
they turned that into a whatyoucall, a rehabilitation place, you
know?"

"So then, back here, huh?" Balzic said, sipping at his beer.

"Yup. Pinned-up sleeve and a Purple Heart and a disability
check every month for as long as I live."

"And then this place, right?"

"No, no. I had this place before the war. Went way out on a
limb in thirty-eight. Way out. . . . It ain't a bad life. Course, I
never had much ambition. Just so I make enough to take care of
my mother and have enough left over to pay for my Steeler
tickets."

"You on that bandwagon, huh?" Balzic said.

"Hey, I been watching the Steelers since they were using the
single wing. I had season tickets since 1947. I ain't on no bandwagon. I watched the Steelers lose football games every way you
could think of and I never bitched. And I ain't no gambler
neither. Never bet a penny on a football game. I just used to go
to old Forbes Field every Sunday when the Steelers were home
and it just brought out a lot of emotion in me I couldn't get rid
of no other way.

"Those aren't high school kids down there; those are men.
Giants. And they're down there strugglin' and sweatin' and
bleedin' and doin' a little war right there between those chalk
stripes on the grass and I just found out I could whoop and holler
my guts out and nobody would think I was nuts. It didn't make
no difference to anybody else what I was really hollering about.
People around me were all hollering too. I mean, it really helps

you, brother, to reach down to your toes and pull out a yell you been keepin' bottled up inside you for Christ knows how long.

"And I'm telling you the truth, that's why I started goin'," Ripulsky said. "Just to holler my ass off. And then a funny thing happened. I started to really like the game. And the less I needed to whoop and holler, the more I liked the game. And nobody around here believes me when I tell 'em, but I don't give a shit who wins. I only cared about that when I first started goin', 'cause then the Steelers couldn't win for losin' and I really liked to go watch guys struggle their asses off and still get whipped — which is what they used to do then. All the time. I felt like one of 'em. Like one of the goddamn linemen, nobody knows their names, they'd work their ass off and no matter what they did they'd still get beat and, oh, I used to holler. I used to scream and a lotta people thought I was screamin' at them. But I wasn't. I was screamin' for how they must've felt 'cause that's how I felt."

"You still scream and holler when you go to the games?"

"Oh yeah, every once in a while I reach down and bring one up, but now it's just 'cause yellin' makes me feel so good. I tell you, yellin' is almost as good for you as laughin' — there's nothin' as good for you as that, no sir, laughin's the real elixir, but hollerin' comes close."

"I never heard it explained like this before," Balzic said.

"Oh, it's no big deal. I just sat down and figured why the hell I was payin' good money to watch twenty-two guys knock each other ass over elbows, and that was it. But when you get around the so-called fans, why, you have to talk all the bullshit about statistics and point spreads and how come the Steelers did this on third down and how come they didn't do that, and if you're goin' to get along with the people that sit around you, you have to go along with 'em and go through the words. I never understood that, but then I figured they were talking all that strategy and stuff for the same reason I was yellin'. It was something they had to do — it makes 'em feel something that they don't feel every day in what they do.

"But, shit, all I watch is the struggle down there in the pits.

Those fuckin' elephants down there with no names. Hell, half the time I don't even know what happened to the ball. I just watch 'em bullin' up their necks and takin' off at one another. . . . Boy, I really been beatin' your ears about this, huh?" Ripulsky said, blushing. "Shit, I don't get much chance to talk about this."

"That's all right. I understand," Balzic said. "Besides, I never heard anybody talk about football that way."

"You're not a fan, huh?"

"No, no, that I'm not. All football is to me is traffic problems at the high school games."

"Well, some time you want to go shout and holler and jump up and down and just carry on like an idiot and not get put in a straitjacket, you think about goin' to see the Steelers play. I mean it. It'll get rid of some tension, boy, it'll just slide right off like petroleum jelly, I'm tellin' you."

"I'll keep it in mind," Balzic said, laughing.

"Uh, say," Ripulsky said, "were you, uh, were you on the level before about Jimmy Romanelli and his wife and her father, huh? There isn't something else, is there?"

"No, there's nothing else."

"I mean, I don't mean to stick into your business," Ripulsky said, "but you got to admit it's a little funny that the chief of police takes all the trouble you're taking over something that ain't even happened yet, you know?"

"Well," Balzic said, "no matter how funny it looks, that's all there is to it. Nothing has happened yet — I mean, nothing official, but I've talked to Frances a couple of times and I guess there's something in me that remembers when she was a little girl and I used to watch her so my father could talk to her father.

"You should've heard those conversations — one Italian accent and one Serbian. I never knew what the hell they were talking about — the mines, I guess, I really don't know. But you didn't have to know what they were talking about to know they really understood one another and really respected each other — at least that's what I always thought.

"The only other things they had in common was they both loved wine and they both loved those peppers. God, I don't know how they ate those things. They'd sit out there for hours and eat those things." Balzic suddenly straightened up and downed the last of his beer.

"You leavin'? Hey, come on, have another beer. On the house."

"No, thanks. Another time. I got to satisfy myself about something or I'm going to have it buggin' me until I do." Balzic walked out with a wave over his shoulder.

He called the station from his cruiser and asked Lynch to locate Officer Russell from the state Bureau of Drug Enforcement and have him call on the radio. Balzic turned the car around and was heading back out of the patch when Russell called.

"Hey, Muddio, what you need, paisan?"

"You know those guys you told me about the other day, the ones who move the goods and, uh, hang out at the spaghetti house with no name?"

"Certainly I remember. That's our livest number."

"Those guys out there at this time of day?"

"Hey, Mario, what d'you got in mind?"

"At ease, Russell, I ain't goin' to go fuckin' around in your investigation. I just want to see who these people are, see what they look like, see how my interest fits in with their style — if he does, and so forth and so on."

"Oh your interest fits in there all right. Romanelli was with them last night when they got back from their travels."

"Oh yeah? What time was that?"

"One A.M. He was with them until two at which time he departed with a package. Where he went after he went to a house not his home last night is anybody's guess."

"What's that mean?"

"It means one of our people followed him and he went to a house not his own house, and we don't know where he went from there. Our man was afraid of being spotted. It's pretty hard to be cool following somebody at that time of night in that coal patch, you know?"

"But you do know it wasn't to his own house?"

"That we do."

"That's interesting," Balzic said.

"We think so."

"Well, thank you, Russell. I appreciate it. And I promise not to fuck around with your principals."

"Please don't. We got a ton of time in on this one. I'd hate to lose it now. Especially over some corollary thing."

"Over some 'corollary' thing? God, you drug guys are really smart. You use all those big words."

"Up yours, Muddio. G'bye. I got work to do."

"Hey, me to! What d'you think I'm doin' here? Wasting tax-payers' money, you —" It was a waste of breath because Russell had clicked off.

Balzic drove to the spaghetti house with no name. It was on the road out of Rocksburg toward Bovard Township, a twisty, two-lane blacktop with some houses here and there in clusters and some trailers, also in clusters, and hardwoods at roadside and an occasional field recently plowed.

The spaghetti house shared an intersection with a gas station, a soft ice cream stand, and a convenience food store. Why these four businesses had been put on these four corners was anybody's guess.

What immediately caught Balzic's eye as he pulled into the gravel parking lot of the spaghetti house was the number of large rental trucks parked at the side of the gas station. There were several small trailers and one van, which might have been ex-pected. What surprised Balzic was that there were four enclosed trucks capable of hauling four- or six-ton loads.

There was one car parked in the lot of the spaghetti house, a plain-looking four-door sedan. There were no other vehicles in sight, none at the gas station, none at the soft ice cream stand, none in front of the convenience store. It was puzzling because Balzic knew there were several large housing developments within a mile or two in any of four directions, not to mention a couple of coal patches.

More puzzling to Balzic was the sound of several male voices laughing and bantering as he opened the door to the bar of the spaghetti house. As he walked into the bar, a horseshoe affair with soft lights, thick, black, vinyl-covered padding for the elbow rests on the bar, and stools backed in the same thick, black vinyl, the laughter almost petered out.

There were four young men seated at the bend of the horseshoe opposite the door Balzic came in and an elderly, grayish, baldish man in a white shirt and a white apron behind the bar.

The laughter and banter slowed for a moment and then continued as before. The bartender approached as Balzic sat four stools away from the nearest of the young men, and he placed a circular, cardboard coaster on the bar. "Yes sir."

"Beer, please. Draft if you have it."

"I have," the man said in a heavy Italian accent. It took Balzic a few moments of concentration, but he knew as he watched the old man pour the beer that he was Gerry Tripoli, the owner.

"Mr. Tripoli," Balzic said, extending his hand over the bar, "it *is* you, isn't it?"

"Yes . . . yes. Who are you?" The man set down the beer, wiped his hands on his apron and took Balzic's hand tentatively.

"Mario Balzic. Remember me?"

"Oh for God's sake, sure. How you doin'? I no see you for longa time, my God. What happened with you, huh?"

"Oh, I don't know. Just quit coming around, I guess."

The conversation at the bend of the horseshoe stopped.

"So. Huh? So whata you tink — you gonna come back, eata something, huh? Bringa you family, huh?"

"You still making the sauce?"

"Oh yeah. Alla time. Nobody else can teach. I stilla make. Sure."

"Well, for sure I'll be back. I'll bring my family."

"Sure. That'sa right. Ho-boy. Son of a gunsky. What you tink, huh? Hey, you stilla cop? Huh?"

"Yeah. Still a cop. Chief of police now in Rocksburg."

"Chief! Ho-boy. How do you likea dat? Chief!" The old man slapped his hand on the bar each time he said "chief." "How longa you been chief, huh?"

"Oh, long time now. Ten, eleven years now. I forget really. It's at least eleven years."

"Hey. You catcha lotta crooks, huh? Likea televis, huh. Huh?" The old man's laugh was at once impish and teasing. He tapped Balzic on the right hand. "Shoota too? Huh?"

Balzic shook his head no. "Hell, no. I don't even carry a gun. They scare me. Nah, mostly all I do is take care of traffic and parking and once in a while we get some people who had too much to drink, you know. Or they're playing their music too loud or something like that."

"No shoot?"

"No shoot," said Balzic, laughing.

"No catcha crooks?"

"Oh, you know, once in a while." Balzic looked over at the four young men who were making no attempt to hide their interest in the conversation. "Once in a while, we get a wise guy or two. They don't last too long. You know why?" Balzic turned back to look at the old man.

"Huh? Why?"

" 'Cause they always brag. They always shoot their mouths off. They always got to tell somebody how they managed to get away with this or how they foxed that guy or how they know how to do something. And what's funny is — they always get mad at the guy who talks to the cops. But they never get mad at themselves, even though if they hadn't bragged so much in the first place nobody would ever know anything to tell the cops. You know what I mean, Mr. Tripoli?"

"Yes," Mr. Tripoli said, nodding soberly. "I know."

"I thought you'd know what I meant," Balzic said, taking a long swallow of his beer. "Now you take this fella I been after for the last couple days."

"You after somebody anow? Huh? Ina here?"

"No, no, Mr. Tripoli. I just stopped in."

"Oh."

There was suppressed laughter at the bend of the horseshoe.

"Well, this fella, he can't help but brag about what he's doing. And who do you think he brags to? To his wife, that's who. And that would be okay, 'cause every man's always trying to tell his wife he's more important than she thinks. But this fella's trying to brag to the same wife he's been beating up. And now there she is with a grudge against him and she knows he's got all this money and he tells her he's winning it playin' cards and she knows that's a lot of crap because she knows he's a lousy card player. And yet there he is, with all these twenty-dollar bills, and there she is, with these bruises on her face. And who do you think she's startin' to talk to?"

The old man looked up at Balzic from under his brows. "You?"

"Me," Balzic said, nodding. "And you know what?"

"Uh-uh."

"Well, the next time he bangs her around I'm gonna do a nasty thing to him. I'm gonna go arrest him and then I'm gonna take him to a magistrate who's a real good friend of mine and I'm gonna whisper something to that magistrate and he's gonna set the bond so high on this fella that it's gonna take all this fella's cash to stay out of jail. And he's gonna be really unhappy about that. And you know what some people will do, Mr. Tripoli, to stay out of jail?"

"No. What?"

Until that moment Balzic had not been sure that the man was putting him on. Now he was sure. And so he continued to talk slowly as though explaining to a child what any child would already know.

"Well, Mr. Tripoli, I know you'll find this hard to believe, but every time people find out they're really for sure, for absolute certain goin' to jail, they start to do the damnedest things. They mostly start lookin' around to see if they can make a trade for freedom. And some people'll trade anything. Anything."

"No kiddin'."

"Yeah," Balzic said, nodding as ponderously as he could make himself. He thought he was probably laying it on too thick, but what the hell. Until now, he'd never known this old man to have aspired to be anything but the owner of a no-name restaurant on a remote intersection of two township roads. And this old bastard, Balzic thought, looking in Tripoli's eyes and smiling stupidly, was probably the brains for those four movers and shakers at the bend of the horseshoe.

"What'sa dis fella's name, maybe I know?"

"Oh I don't think you know him. He lives over in Kennedy Township, clear on the other side of Rocksburg." God, Balzic thought, I'm making it sound as though it's halfway across the state; it can't be four miles from here. I better knock it off. Nobody's as stupid as I'm playing.

"I know somea people live there. Ya, sure. Who'sa dis guy? You can tell."

Balzic tried to make it look as though he was debating with himself. He shook his head. "I probably shouldn't be talking any more about this, Mr. Tripoli. It wouldn't be fair to the guy. I mean, even if he is beating up his wife and lyin' to her, tellin' her he's gettin' the money one way and she knows he's getting it some other way. It wouldn't be fair. And when it comes to trial — if it comes to trial — and somebody finds out I was telling about him and using his name, why, shit, I'd really get in lots of trouble. The case'd probably get thrown out.

"But you know the terrible thing about this, Mr. Tripoli?"

"No, what?"

"Can I have another beer, please?"

"Sure. Finish. I give 'nother one."

Balzic drained his glass, turned his head toward the four movers and shakers, and let loose a slow belch. "Excuse me," he said to them, making his eyelids droop ever so slightly for a split second.

Tripoli took the glass away, filled it, and returned. " 'At's okay. No money. On me."

"Thank you," Balzic said, and made himself weave the tiniest bit. "Where was I? Oh. The terrible part."

"Ya. Thata part."

"This fella's using all kinds of dope. Yeah." Balzic nodded slowly and then shook his head.

"Dope?" The old man bent his head forward to peer in Balzic's eyes. "What kinda dope?"

"Two kinds. Something to speed him up. And then something to slow him down. His wife says sometimes he's like walkin' on the walls. And other times she says it's like he's drunk only she can't smell booze on his breath. Whatta you think of that, huh? Here in the coal patches, huh? Dope. Jesus Christ."

The old man shook his head and made tsking and clucking sounds. "I tella you, thata dope, that'sa everyplace. I'ma no kiddin'. It'sa everyplace. You can't turn around no more, somebody's atry to sell you thata stuff. It's a goddamna sin, you know?"

"That's just what it is, Mr. Tripoli. A goddamn sin. It's a gluttony, that's what it is. A form of gluttony."

There were suppressed titters and swallowed guffaws and fits of coughing at the bend of the horseshoe.

Balzic staggered backward off the stool a half step and quickly regained his balance. He took up his glass and emptied it and set it down with a bang on the bar. "Mr. Tripoli, you take care of yourself," Balzic said, swaying forward and extending his hand. "It's been really good to see you again after all these years."

"You too," Tripoli said, taking Balzic's hand and shaking it with both his hands.

"You just keep on makin' sauce, thats' good stuff to make."

"Ya, and you, youa better stopa drink today, you know?" Tripoli released Balzic's hand and waved his finger at him as though admonishing a little boy. "I tink you havea too much now, no?"

"I have too much, yes," Balzic said and smiled dully. Without another word, he turned and walked out of the bar, stepping nearly as far to the side as to the front with each step.

He heard somebody following him and so he maintained his drunken gait until he was behind the wheel of the cruiser. He pretended not to notice as one of the movers and shakers stepped around the front of the car and came up to the driver's window. He also tried not to appear too startled to see the mover and shaker there when he looked up.

"Hey, pal, tell me something," the fellow said. He was very young, hardly out of his teens, with an indolent face and a wisp of a moustache.

"What?" Balzic said.

"You no shit the chief of police? In Rocksburg?"

Balzic nodded.

"And you don't carry a gun?"

Balzic nodded again.

The young mover and shaker with the indolent expression threw back his head and shook with laughter. He laughed for fully ten seconds and then he bent down and put his face close to Balzic's and said, "Well, tell me, Chief, just what the fuck do you do when somebody don't pay attention, huh? What do you do then, I mean, how do you get their attention?"

"C'mere and I'll show you," Balzic said, putting his left hand on the window knob and edging his right hand slowly toward the window while still keeping it on the steering wheel.

"What?"

"C'mere and I'll show you," Balzic said again.

When the mover and shaker bent his head close to the open window, his eyes still teary from laughter, Balzic's right hand shot out and caught him by the hair at the same time as his left hand wound up the window until the mover and shaker was pinned to the top of the door by the window across his throat and was gasping for breath and trying desperately to say something.

"What do I do to get somebody's attention, huh? Is that what you said, numbnuts? Huh? I do this, that's what I do. And then," said Balzic, starting the cruiser and putting it in gear, "and then, asshole, I take them for a ride. And believe me, I always get their attention when the car starts moving."

The mover and shaker's voice began somehow to function and he made squealing sounds and his eyes rolled wildly from side to side.

Balzic snapped off the parking brake and let the automatic transmission creep the car backward away from the building. He let it move almost a foot before he applied the brakes.

Then, putting his face close to the swelling red face of the mover and shaker, he said, "The day I need a gun to deal with assholes like you, sonny, that's the day I go see when my retirement checks start."

Balzic wound down the window quickly and shoved the head outward, sending the mover and shaker flying to the gravel on his pants where he rolled over on his back and coughed and hacked and wheezed to get air.

Balzic backed slowly out of the parking lot and drove back off toward Rocksburg, looking in the rearview mirror to see one of the other movers and shakers run to the side of the one on the ground.

Balzic had a terrible time resisting the urge to spin the car around and go wheeling back at them at about forty-five or fifty miles per hour and then do a skid stop and cover them with dust and dirt. Nah, he thought. Be my luck to hit one of 'em in the face with a piece of gravel and really hurt him and then I *would* be checking to see when my retirement checks start. Shit. Well, you can't have everything.

Balzic called the station and got Lynch, the desk sergeant who didn't want to be one.

"You still there?" Balzic asked.

"Hell yes I'm still here."

"What's the word from upstairs?"

"The word from upstairs is you better get your ass back up there where it belongs and that's the exact words of the mayor."

"They didn't settle anything?"

"From what the mayor says, the only thing they agree on is that you ain't where you're supposed to be."

"My ass," Balzic said. "You got anything else of interest? Huh? A double homicide maybe?"

"No. Nutsy Turrell was in here a little while ago, says he poisoned the water again."

"He's hoping one day he'll say that and somebody'll take him out and show him where the reservoir is. When he was a little kid he used to tell everybody he swam in there every day and pissed in it and we were all drinking his piss. We believed him too, until we found out he didn't know where the damn thing was. What else?"

"Old man Johnson's lost again."

"D'you put the word out to the troops?"

"Yeah."

"D'you tell 'em not to take him to the mental health clinic, to take him home?"

"Yeah. But I think he ought to be in the mental health, myself that is. I mean I think he ought to —"

"I know what you think. We been over this before. There's nothing crazy about him. He just wanders around. Lots of old people do that. You know that as well as I do. You're gonna do it if you live long enough and so am I. You hope some smart-ass cop hauls you off to the mental health clinic every time you decide to go for a walk? Huh? And forget where you are? Huh?"

"No. I hope they fuckin' shoot me, I get like that."

"Yeah, sure. Right. Hey, type up a memo and pass it out to the troops. Maybe some of 'em'll still be on the force when you're wandering around without your pants or your shoes on the wrong feet. I'm sure there'll be some gun-happy asshole who'll oblige you. Anything else?"

"That woman called again. About her husband. He still ain't come home."

"What'd you tell her?"

"I told her you were workin' on it."

"I am — in my own way. Sort of. What kind of shape's she in? Sound all right?"

"She was swearin' a lot."

"At you? Me? Us? Or just generally?"

"Generally."

"That's something, I guess. So? What else?"

"Oh shit, I almost forgot. Warden down at Southern Regional says he got a man wants to talk to you about a whole lot of things."

"What man?"

"Somebody named Brown. I wrote it down here —"

"Beryl?"

"Yeah, that's it."

"Forget it. Beryl Brown's been trying to sell me information for ten years. He's full of shit. He doesn't have anything ever. All he's trying to do is snuggle up to me 'cause one time I told him if I ever caught him in town I was gonna kill his black ass and put a little automatic in his palm."

"Why'd you want to do that?"

"Don't you know him? Huh? Boots Brown?"

"Oh oh oh, yeah, that Brown. Okay. I know. Somebody ought to do that to that sonofabitch. Why didn't ya?"

"He never came to town, I guess. Least I never saw him. Well, we can quit using the airways, Harry."

"Why?"

"I just parked outside the building. I think we can finish our conversation inside."

"Oh."

Balzic parked the cruiser and walked into the duty room on the lookout for faces at the windows of the second-floor conference room. Having seen none on the way into the building, he thought he had it made for a dash to his office, but he walked into the duty room just as Mayor Bellotti and Solicitor Renaldo came in from the other corridor.

"Where you been, Mario?" Bellotti said.

"I've been sick, throwing up, diarrhea, all that good stuff. I been home."

"No, you haven't," Renaldo said.

"What does that mean?" Balzic said.

"That means you haven't been home. It's a straightforward, simple statement of fact. You have not been at your residence."

"Says who?"

"Says your mother, that's who," Renaldo said.

"Hey," Balzic said, walking very quickly up to the solicitor and putting his face near the solicitor's. "You buggin' my mother, huh?"

"We simply called her. Nobody is bugging your mother," Renaldo said, drawing away.

"Who the fuck told you to call her? Huh? Who the —"

"Mario! For crying out loud," Bellotti said, "take it easy. Slow down."

"— who the fuck told you to go botherin' my mother about anything, you shiny-ass goddamn shyster you? Huh?"

"Mario, it was a simple phone call. That's all it was," Bellotti chanted soothingly — or tried to.

"Get your finger out of my face, Mr. Mayor," Balzic said. "You two guys pay attention. You don't ever bug my mother about anything I do or do not do — is that understood? I mean, you both understand that?"

"Mario," Bellotti protested as charmingly as he could manage, "nobody is bothering your mother. She's a lovely person and very dear to me —"

"Not by a goddamn mile as dear as she is to me."

"— I understand that, Mario, but we need you in — you have to understand, we need you upstairs to resolve some very difficult problems —"

"Oh will you stop trying to pump sunshine up my ass, Angelo? Will you?"

"By all means," Renaldo said.

Balzic took a step closer to Renaldo and began to talk very low, through just partly open teeth. "Hey, you listen to me, Solicitor. I've taken an oath to uphold the law of the nation, the commonwealth, the county, and the city. And that oath means everything there is and if you can't figure out what *everything* means, that *everything* means I put my ass on the line! I mean, if it comes right down to it, I got to put my ass right out there in front! And as long as that's what it means to carry my shield around then no weasel-faced motherfucker like you is going to bug my mother about where I am or where I ain't! Ever!"

"Mario," Bellotti said, stepping between Balzic and Renaldo and trying to say something calming and quiet. "It was a mistake, a blunder on our part, for which we — I — for which I am genuinely sorry. Please accept my apologies."

"I do believe the chief of police is making threatening gestures and his tone and expression have all been threatening," Renaldo said, stepping farther away. "All of which constitutes a simple assault on my person."

"No shit!" Balzic shouted. "No shit! Tell me the law. Go 'head! Tell it to me. And add this to it, you hear me! You ever call my mother again and worry her about where I'm supposed to be, I'll break the finger you dial the phone with. And I'll break the hand and the arm and the shoulder! How's that, Solicitor? That enough of an assault on your person, huh? Go call her right now. Go on! So I can start breaking your bones."

Renaldo turned and looked at Patrolman Harry Lynch, the reluctant desk sergeant. "I want the chief of police placed under arrest."

Lynch showed no emotion. "No sir. I don't think so."

"What? Why not?"

"Sir, you're an officer of the city just the same as I am. If you want him arrested, you can do it."

"Not physically I can't," Renaldo said. "I am asking your assistance. I demand your assistance!"

"Sir, you don't need my assistance. You're not in any danger."

"He's threatening me! By word, by tone, by expression, by his advancement toward me."

"Sir, you know the law better'n me, but I think you're forgettin' what you know," Lynch said. "Simple assault won't cost the chief here more than fifteen dollars and costs in front of magistrates that he knows better than anybody around here. And they're gonna suspend the sentences anyway. So all it's gonna mean is fifteen or twenty minutes out of his life to go to the hearing, which is what it will cost you. Do you see where I'm going?"

Balzic had to stand back and look admiringly at Harry Lynch. For a street cop with no administrative ambitions, Lynch was handling a lawyer — the city solicitor no less — like he'd been doing it for years.

"I still want him arrested."

"Sir, I've already told you you can do it yourself and I've also told you that it will wind up costing you as much as it's gonna cost him. 'Cause see, sir, if you arrest him or if I arrest him, either way I gotta testify and my testimony's gonna be simple assault, nothing more. And we're back where we started."

"What's your name, Sergeant?" Renaldo said.

"His name is Lynch," Balzic said before Lynch could reply, "and he's not a sergeant, he's a patrolman who's acting as a sergeant because somebody promoted one of our three desk sergeants to lieutenant and forced me to put this patrolman in a place he doesn't want to be. And you fuck with him and I'll consider that the same as buggin' my mother about where I am."

Mayor Bellotti threw up his hands. "Oh for God's sake, this is ridiculous, we're all acting like children here —"

"Hey," Balzic said, "I didn't promote Clemente. You two did. And I know why and you know why and we all know that we know. The only one who doesn't know is Clemente. So get off my back, get off Lynch's back, and don't call my mother goddamnit! And if there was a childish move, promotin' Clemente was it. You want me upstairs? Fine. But don't expect me to sit still for the bullshit. I'm leaving. And every time the bullshit starts, I'm gonna leave.

"The issues upstairs are simple: the men want more money, they want more money for court time, they want more time off, they want one of their own on the pension board to make sure they don't get screwed by some C.P.A. Those are reasonable requests. How it's taken you guys three fuckin' weeks to not even get around to one of them is what's ridiculous. It's worse. It's a motherfucking sin. And I ain't gonna be part of it.

"I can't look my men in the face knowing how much time's being wasted on nothin'. These things should've been done in a week. Eight days at the outside. And we haven't got around to anything."

"We settled the problem of the number of officers assigned to motor patrol," Bellotti said.

"Oh stop it, Angelo. We did that — no, I did that this morning 'cause if I let that turkey go on for five more minutes, I was gonna be sick."

"I thought you said you *were* sick," Renaldo said.

"Oh for crissake, Renaldo, will you wise up? Huh? I keep telling you this town don't roll over just 'cause you guys wanna negotiate a contract."

"Well, which is it — were you sick or not?"

"Oh why don't you go get bent around a pole someplace, huh?"

"Come on, men. Gentlemen. Christ almighty," Bellotti said, looking first at the ceiling and then at his feet. "Can we have something resembling a civil discussion!"

"I can be civil with anybody," Balzic said. "All they gotta do is not bug my mother and not get on my men."

"And all the chief has to do is to be where he's supposed to be," Renaldo said, "and to avoid threats either by word, expression, or gesture. But it doesn't matter whether he acts in a civilized and responsible manner in the future, I give you my word I will not forget what threats were made here today."

Balzic groaned and walked away toward his office.

"Mario," Bellotti said, "where you going now?"

"I got heartburn. I'm goin' to get some stuff for it."

"How unfortunate," Renaldo said, "the chief of police has an upset tum-tum. My my."

"Fuck you, Renaldo."

"And his curses are so wildly imaginative."

Balzic spun about. "You want a good curse? Huh? How about this one? I hope that no matter what happens to you, I hope you can't smell it, taste it, or fuck it. I hope —"

"Mario, that's enough!" the mayor said. "I mean it now, that's enough. You're really saying some, uh, some — you're gonna have a hard time trying to get over this, uh, this what you're saying here."

"Nothing to it," Balzic said, turning and going back to his office where, while he rooted through his desk with one hand for the antacid tablets, he phoned his mother with the other to satisfy himself that she knew he was all right and that Renaldo's call hadn't alarmed her. She said she knew, of course, that he was all right and she said, further, that nothing Renaldo could say would alarm her because everyone knew he dishonored all parents because of the way he treated his own. Thus satisfied, Balzic found the antacid tablets, popped two into his mouth, and walked out into the duty room wondering if Ripulsky hadn't been right about going to football games to holler and shout and carry on like a fool to get rid of emotion. Hell, anything had to be better than exchanging snide cracks with Renaldo. Even football.

Balzic walked past Lynch and then Renaldo and then the mayor, and before anyone could say a word, he was out the door and running to his cruiser. He pulled out of the parking lot and saw the mayor in the rearview mirror standing on the steps and looking very frustrated indeed. "He's your whore, Angelo," Balzic said under his breath. "You go to bed with him. But if he calls my mother again, I will break his index finger. Both of them. Somebody ought to do it out of respect for his father, poor old bastard. He puts that shit through law school and then gets treated like garbage. No father should have a son like Renaldo. Better to have a daughter who's a whore than a son who's like Renaldo, takes everything you give him and then spits on you 'cause you can't talk English without an accent . . . Jesus Keerist."

For hours Balzic hid in the cruiser. Sometimes he drove and sometimes he parked by the Conemaugh River and sat and stared at the water, but mostly he drove, knowing that there was no situation that might come up that he wouldn't learn about as soon as anybody else. After a while he was laughing silently at himself because he knew that when he was hiding like this — on the mouse, a dope dealer expressed it once — he was not much different from some hoods he'd known. They lived in their cars. Someplace they had a room, a place to keep the clothes they weren't wearing, but their home was in their cars. And the rooms they had were usually in motels, with the car parked just on the other side of some glass, where they could go and pull the drapes back periodically and look at their car, their mobility, their badge of success, their manhood, their contempt for what they believed was most square — a home in a structure that didn't move, that was attached to the dirt, to the community, the state, the nation, the planet, a home that meant that one was attached as surely as the structure was.

Not all hoodlums were like this. Only some. And every time Balzic fled from his responsibilities as he was doing now, sooner or later it would occur to him that he was as contemptuous in his way of square things and square ways as the most contemptuous of those hoods he knew. And then he would laugh at himself and think how often he had found himself in situations where only craziness could be counted on to get him through successfully. Then he'd think further how only a second's miscalculation and the craziness he counted on to get him through successfully might not. And if it didn't, then instead of becoming a private memory it became a public record of failed craziness. And one thing a chief of police could not live with was failed craziness. Nobody would let him.

Twice in one day, in less than an hour, he'd indulged his craziness. The first time was in the parking lot at the spaghetti house with no name when that young mover and shaker had followed him out and taunted him. And he had decided what to do at almost the same instant he felt himself doing it, and even while he was doing it he knew that there had been nothing in him but a feeling, an intuition, that that kid didn't have a pistol. Because if the kid had been armed with a pistol, Balzic knew that it could have been just as easily himself lying in the parking lot as the kid. He could sit now in the car and rationalize all he wanted about checking the kid out visually as he walked around the front of the car. But he had not seen the kid's back or right hip or either of his legs below the knees, and yet Balzic had gone ahead with the craziness that got him through successfully. Looking back on it, and knowing that because he could not truly say that the kid wasn't armed, it was one of the stupider things he'd ever done. All it had really done was satisfy him emotion-ally.

Which is what he got for screaming at Renaldo and Bellotti. Emotional satisfaction was hardly worth what they could do to him if they put their minds to it. Not Bellotti so much, because Bellotti went about his business by storing favors and then calling them in. Renaldo, Balzic thought, Renaldo was another matter. Renaldo stored wounds. He squirreled away insults and innuendos and insinuations and inferences and came back at his enemies with a briefcase full of documented revenge and a heart full of mean glee.

Shouting at Renaldo, threatening him, was really dumb, Balzic thought. Satisfying as hell, but really dumb. Because while the young movers and shakers were dangerous, they were physically dangerous. and Balzic had trained all his adult life to respond to physical danger. But Renaldo didn't have to lay a finger on you. All City Solicitor Renaldo needed was a typewriter and a blank fitness report. And what's worse, Balzic knew Renaldo would always be trying to even things as long as he remained city solicitor.

"Sometimes I can be bright," Balzic said aloud, "and sometimes I can be brave. I wonder if I ever been both at once? Shit. I wonder if I knew it if I was?"

It was dark when Balzic finally went back to the station. He had been home for a couple of hours to see his family and to eat, but except for that time he had stayed away from Bellotti and Renaldo and company, following everything that went on — which wasn't much — over the radio in his car or the monitor in his home.

Old man Johnson had been found and returned to his residence — he tried to give the beat officer who drove him home a quarter tip — and Nutsy Turrell still had not located the city reservoir. Nutsy, too, had been returned to his residence where he spit on the beat cop who returned him and kicked his own brother in the shins.

Desk Sergeant Vic Stramsky was on the phone when Balzic

walked in, and he motioned for Balzic to hurry up. By the expression on Stramsky's face Balzic could tell that Stramsky wanted greatly to be relieved of a nuisance.

When Balzic picked up an extension phone he knew why. It was Frances Romanelli.

"That's about the fifth time she called just since I came on," Stramsky said. "I think I know why the guy ain't coming home."

Balzic shrugged at Stramsky and said hello.

"Is this you?"

"I'm me if that's what you mean. Balzic. It's me."

"Oh, thank God. Where were you — oh never mind. Those guys you got working for you, they really don't care — uh, they can really get snippy and snotty."

"Look, Frances, the guys who work the phones in here, the dispatchers, they got to listen to some weird stuff at times, so unless the person calling has a real problem, they tend not to worry about it or pay too much attention to it —"

"Does that mean you think I don't have a *real* problem?"

"I didn't say that. What I —"

"My husband is still not home and — oh Jesus I hate myself when I think I'm carrying on."

"Look, uh, to be perfectly honest about this thing, it still hasn't been twenty-four hours since your husband left —"

"It's been two days! Longer! Almost three."

"No no, Frances. He was home last night. I talked to him, you talked to him, we all talked to each other, such as it was. So when you call in here and ask for help, the man with the duty in here, he doesn't classify your problem as a priority thing, you understand me? Huh?"

"I understand you. Do you understand me? I am some place I never been before. I don't know what I'm feeling. And when I do know what I'm feeling, I'm so scared — oh please, please, come and talk to me. Please. Nobody talks to me. Nobody thinks I have a problem. I could scream. The ladies at the community college are telling me all different things. I don't know who to believe." She was sobbing now and couldn't speak.

"Okay, Frances, you hang on and I'll be out and we'll sit

down and drink a little wine maybe and see if we can't make a little sense, okay? Huh? Okay?"

She muttered something that sounded like agreement and Balzic hung up. He told Stramsky where he was going and left.

In fifteen minutes he was out of the car and going down the short walk and she was peeking at him over the bottom of the small window in the front door and then opening the door.

As he stepped inside she fell against him and began to weep. Balzic closed the door and put his arms around her and patted her shoulder and swayed with her as though rocking a child.

At last, after many minutes had passed, she eased away from him and made her way haltingly to a box of tissues on the dining table. She wiped her face and blew her nose and got more tissue and blew her nose again. She smiled at him with swollen eyes.

"We must've really had something going when you used to come here with your father," she said. "I haven't felt this good about — uh, about anybody in a long time. And I think it's 'cause I must've really trusted you back then, you know?"

"Yeah. Well, I used to look out for you, make sure you didn't get hurt, and I guess I carried you around a lot."

"You used to bring me stuff, too."

"Yeah? I did? What kind of stuff?"

"I just remember two things. Once you brought me a little doll made out of a sock —"

"Oh yeah, yeah — my mother used to make them and give 'em to the Red Cross. She made 'em out of men's work socks. I remember."

"I loved that doll. I had it, oh I don't know, a long time. But I can't remember what happened to it." She started to laugh and cry at the same time, two bursts of laugh-sobs. And then she quit and blushed.

"And what was the other thing?"

"The other thing you used to bring me all the time was those little bottles of wax with the real sweet, oh, it was like pop, only it wasn't pop. They were supposed to be bottles of pop, remember? They were only about this big." She held her thumb and index finger less than two inches apart.

"I remember."

"You'd bite off the top and drink the stuff, it was real sweet and was orange or cherry, and then you'd chew the wax, remember?"

"Yeah. We used to stop over at Cremanese's Market to get them. My dad always bought them for me. And he'd tell me to save one for you. You got a heckuva memory. You were just a little girl."

"Oh, I remembered that. I forgot it all these years, but it came back to me when you started talking about your father and mine . . . boy, everything was easy then, huh?"

"Yeah. Pretty easy. No more though, huh, Frances?"

"God, I . . . sometimes I don't think I'm gonna last till Saturday. Other times, boy, I don't honest to God think I'm gonna make it till tomorrow and when I say tomorrow I mean one minute after midnight. Hey, why don't you sit down — you don't have to stand up all night."

Balzic nodded and took a chair at the dining table.

"You want something, huh? Coffee? What d'you want? I probably won't have it, all I got to drink, alcohol, you know, is a couple cans of beer in the refrigerator. You want one of them?"

"That'll be fine. I'd like a beer."

She hurried away and hurried back and put the can, opened, and a glass on the table in front of him.

As Balzic poured the beer, she said, "Uh, you were really, uh, it was really nice that you come all the way out . . . uh, I know as far as anybody else cares about it, I probably don't really got a — whatta you call it? A priority problem? Huh?"

Balzic nodded. "It's a crummy bureaucrat's word. And when I use it I'm a crummy bureaucrat."

"You are not anything crummy."

"Oh yes I am. When I use words like that I'm among the crummiest bureaucrats I know — and I know a bunch of 'em."

"Anyway . . . anyway, it was really nice of you. I mean it."

"I know you mean it," Balzic said, sipping the beer.

She fiddled with wadded up tissues in her lap. "My father,"

she began, "he used to talk to me all the time. It was never really
— oh, like I hear the kids at the college say — it was never heavy
stuff. Important. We never talked about important stuff. Everything's serious to my father. I never heard my father tell a joke
in my life. Or if he did he sure didn't tell 'em to me.

"And after my mother died, he really got serious. I mean, my
father's like a church. Before mass, you know. A big church.
And you just — you might go in there and talk to other people
but you're not gonna tell jokes. And for sure you don't expect
jokes.

"You expect — I don't know — high ceilings, the roof's way
up there and you know it's no place to start giggling over some
joke. That's my father. He's only five foot three or something
like that, but he always reminded me of high ceilings in a big
church.

"But I could always talk to him, you know?"

"And now you don't even know how he'll act if you say
hello, right?"

"Yes! Right! That's really right! I don't know what — yes I do
too. It's like if I say the wrong thing that ceiling's gonna come
down. Right on my head!"

"And he was never like that before?" Balzic said.

"Oh my God no. Never. I mean washing clothes is serious to
him. Going shopping is serious. You think about it. You plan it.
And when you do it, don't mess around. Planting a garden, my
God, there ain't — isn't — nothing more serious than that. He has
the priest come and bless the ground. Yeah. He gives the priest a
bottle of wine and two dollars. It's the same every year. And the
priest comes! And brings holy water and walks all around the
garden sprinkling water and praying.

"I asked the priest once — about ten years ago — it was two
priests ago, I can't even remember his name he was such a dud —
but I asked him if he did that very often and he said he never
done it before but he knew just looking at my father that, when
my father said that's what he wanted him to do, he wasn't gonna
say no. He made the ceremony up. Made up the prayers.

"And I never asked the rest but I think they made 'em up too.

And they always come and it's always the same price. Two dollars and a bottle of wine. And they never complain. Why do you think that is?"

"It's probably 'cause they respect him," Balzic said. "And also because they see he's not foolin' around. He means it."

"Oh he's not foolin' around," Frances said.

"And they can see he means it," Balzic said. "I mean, that's an honest request. Sure as hell, the church got time to bless a garden. That's an honorable blessing. I'm sure that in the farm parishes, the priests all do that all the time in the spring."

"I know, but it's the way they look at him."

"Well, so maybe it's a little rare around here, but anybody could see your father's a serious man. So if you were asked to bless his ground, what the hell, you'd do it even if you had to fake it a little bit."

"Oh I think they all fake it."

"But you can't."

"Huh?"

"You can't fake it with him and you don't even know how you're supposed to think about faking it. You don't know how you think about yourself even thinkin' about fakin' it."

She looked at him and her eyes were growing more puffy by the minute. She nodded quickly several times.

"Well, you got to remember he's an old man. And he's really not from here. He lives here, but he's from a long way from here. And you don't do what you're doing — not where he comes from. It don't matter that he's been here most of his life. In his bones he's still from the old country. And there are —"

"There are some things," she broke in, "you're just not supposed to do."

"Hey, lousy as that sounds, that's right. And there's nothing anybody can do about it. So, you're in a tough place. I mean, you get a couple of those women who burned their brassieres and you bring 'em here and introduce 'em to your father, he'll listen to 'em. He's courteous. He might not even argue with 'em. But when they go away and you say *you're* gonna do it, well, then, it's something else."

"Is it ever." She hung her head.

"I know, I know. But you're his kid, his little girl. And if you don't want to live the way he does, then he thinks that you're saying the way he lives isn't any good. And no matter how many ways you tell him that's not so, he won't believe you.

"It's simple for guys like your father. If what he did was right, then his kids'll want to do it. And if they don't want to do it, then it's because they're ungrateful, disrespectful, got no courtesy or no religion. They're just wrong, that's all. Believe me, Frances, I've seen guys like your father all my life and most of 'em are a pain in the rear to get 'em to understand anything other than what they're used to. It's bad enough with a son, but with a daughter – Jesus, with daughters they're really stoneheads. As nice as they are otherwise. As fair. As honorable. Comes to their daughters they may as well be in fifteenth-century Sicily. What they are is impossible.

"So if you want to change the way you live, you're gonna have to do it in a way that lets him down easy, all the while – and this is the tricky part – knowing that he may not give a damn anyway. He may still go to his grave thinking you're an ungrateful little bitch. And that is tough to take. Believe me, I know what you're dealing with here. And I know how much you wanna make it right. But, Frances, that's still a two-way street. Always has been. And if he don't want to give you room to pass, you know, if he don't wanna do that, well, then it's his problem. And all you gotta do is learn to live with it."

"God, but he's so hard. He don't give me no credit. Oh shit – he doesn't give me any credit."

"Frances, he's a rock. He was always a rock. When my father and your father used to talk out here, what d'you think they used to talk about, huh? The union. The United swear-on-your-mother's-grave-and-get-ready-to-get-your-head-busted Mine Workers. Who do you think was the man here then? Hey, my father was tough. Lots of guys were tough. But your old man, he was a rock.

"My father would be discouraged, losing all his stomach for everything, and he'd come out here and your old man would tell him, 'Fair's fair. Right's right.' And that was that. They could talk all day about strategy and tactics, but in the end it came down to fair is fair and right is right and that was all there was to it. And my old man would go home and get up the next day ready to get his head busted again. And it was all 'cause of your father."

"I know," Frances said. "But how come he don't see fair's fair with me? I mean, it's no different with me. I'm just trying to get what's right for me — what was he trying to get?"

"Hey, I'm not arguing with you. I'm just telling you how he was so you don't forget who you're dealing with."

"Well why am I different?"

"I don't know. All I can tell you is with guys like your father you can't go complicatin' things. Fair's fair in the mines was one thing. That was simple. 'Cause it all came down to whether you were willing to put your butt on the picket line. But there was no question that what you were after was right. You worked in the mine, you busted your can, you deserved to get paid. I mean, you deserved to get paid something more than peanuts. And if you were man enough to dig the coal, then by God you better be man enough to ask for a fair wage. Frances, that was simple."

"But what I want is simple, too," she cried.

"Sure. Sure. I know. But, see, that is not simple to him. What was simple to him was your husband works and you stay home. What your husband does is work. What you do is stay home — two different things."

"I know all this. What do I have to tell him so he'll know it? Jee-suss Christ, I wouldn't be in this shape if Jimmy was still digging coal. It's 'cause the goddamn mine closed that I'm tryin' to do what I'm tryin' to do. What's so hard to understand about that?"

"For me? Nothing. I understand it very clearly. But what you don't understand is that your father does not understand it. You have been — you might have been forced to turn your life upside down because of something outside yourself, but you should've been able to handle it the way you were supposed to handle it. Frances, I don't want to sound like a know-it-all or anything like that, but I think that what your father is really mad about is your husband —"

"Well why doesn't he tell *him* about it? Why is it always me —"

"Because — because, uh, oh hell, I don't know," Balzic said. "Probably because he really doesn't know how to talk to him, to Jimmy."

"But he's not talking to me! It's me — I'm the one he's not talking to."

"I understand that. What I'm sayin' is, he's mad at your husband so he's takin' it out on you. Probably. You follow me?"

She shook her head and went and got more tissues and blew her nose again.

"Boy, he sure got a funny way of goin' about it," she said. "I mean, if he's going to complain about Jimmy why don't he complain to Jimmy? Why's he quit talkin' to me? That's a goofy goddamn way of complainin' to Jimmy."

"I agree," Balzic said. "I agree. I'm not sayin' he's right or he's goin' about it the right way. Hell no. I'm just tellin' you that's probably what he's doin'."

"You think he's really mad at Jimmy? Do you, I mean, no kiddin'?"

Balzic nodded and took a long drink of his beer. He had forgotten about it. "But you come in for it too, you know."

"Why? Why do I come in for it?"

" 'Cause you married him. Out of all the men in the world you picked him. And like the rest, what we talked about before, if you were really a good daughter and loved your father the way you were supposed to, why, hell, you would've married a carbon copy of him. I mean, we know how your father would've acted if he'd been in Jimmy's place. But Jimmy didn't act that way. And you married him. So if you want reasons, there are plenty of reasons. But the principal reason is you picked a husband who turned out not to do things the way your father would've. And that's a helluva reason."

"Oh shit," she said. "Some reason."

"I think it's true."

"I didn't mean that. I think it's true too. I mean it's just a really shitty reason. I mean, how was I supposed to know Jimmy was gonna act like this? He never did before! So how was I supposed to know. You wanna know the truth, Jimmy is a whole lot like my father. A whole lot! And the joke is Jimmy thinks he's really different from my father. But they're a lot alike. They're both stubborn as all hell. And they're never wrong, neither one of 'em. And when something goes wrong, it's my fault! I could be ten miles away and it'd still be my fault."

"You're in a hard place, all right," Balzic said. "I wouldn't trade with you."

"Thanks a lot."

"I wasn't being a wise guy, I was—"

"I know you ain't," she interrupted him. "Aren't." She sighed and her shoulders drooped as the air went out of her. "You know, more and more I wonder just how goddamn important is good English supposed to be — I mean really. How important? At times like this, who cares?"

"You do, or you wouldn't be thinking about it."

"I must, huh?" she said thoughtfully. " 'Cause I been thinkin' about it a lot. It's almost like, when I quit sayin' ain't, I get this funny feelin' a whole lot of things are gonna change. And they're never gonna be the same."

Balzic nodded and finished the beer.

"You want another one? There's only one left."

"Yeah. Why not. But I got to ask you something when you come back."

"Okay," she said and jumped up to get the beer, returning in a moment.

"Uh, Frances, Jimmy's, uh, Jimmy's unemployment checks ran out, right?"

"Sure. A while ago. I can tell you exactly if —"

"No no, it's not important. But, uh, he does have money. Doesn't he?"

"Well, yeah. Sometimes he shows up with money. Like last night."

"But you know he's not making that kind of money playing cards. Or do you?"

"Well he says he is."

"Do you believe him? No. Never mind. Don't answer that. That's a crummy question. I'll just tell you. Jimmy's in a lot of trouble."

"Huh? What kind of trouble?"

"He's being investigated by agents of the state Bureau of Drug Enforcement. Their name's longer than that, but that's good enough."

She frowned and then she giggled nervously. "You're kiddin' me . . . You ain't kiddin' me?"

"No. I'm not. And what I want to ask you is, last night Jimmy was followed into the patch here and, in the words of an agent, he went to 'a house not his own.' Where would that be, Frances?"

"Wait a minute. What're you saying here? That Jimmy's messin' around with — drugs? Is that it?"

Balzic nodded.

"What kind of drugs? What're you — what the hell's goin' on?"

"Just take it easy, Frances, and I'll tell you."

"Please do! I wanna hear!"

"Okay, okay. Jimmy's been seen with some people who are known dealers, movers, of what the state calls controlled substances. Illegal drugs. More than likely marijuana and amphetamines. I don't know this, but I'm guessing because of the way you described him once."

"How did I describe him?" she said, suddenly very defensive.

"You said he looked at times like he was drunk but you couldn't smell booze on his breath and at other times like he was climbing the walls. Is that right? Is he like that?"

"Uh, yeah. Yeah. He's like that. Sometimes." She was growing more defensive by the moment.

"How long's he been acting like that?"

"Whatta you mean, how long?"

"It's a simple question, Frances, how long's he —"

"You say it's simple but I'm thinkin' now maybe it's not so simple." She stood up and backed away from him.

"Frances, sit down and —"

"I'm fine standin' up."

"Okay, then stand up. I'm not after Jimmy for drug use, or possession, or sale, or intent to sell, or conspiracy, or anything else."

"Then why're you talkin' like this?"

"I'm not talkin' like anything. I'm just givin' information. These are facts, Frances. Jimmy's been seen with people, he's been followed, and no doubt photographed, and maybe even recorded. It's all written down in state agents' notebooks. Where he goes, when he arrives, when he departs, who he's with, what changes hands, where he goes after that, what —"

"Stop it! Stop it! You're not trying to help me at all! You're trying to do something to Jimmy! What're you doing this for? I thought I could trust you. I thought I could talk to you —"

"Frances, you are not listening to me —"

"Oh I'm listening all right, I'm really listening. And I don't like what I hear. What a jerk I am!"

Balzic stood up and went toward her, his hands out, imploring her to listen. "Frances, you got it backwards. I think maybe he's in trouble with the guys he's been foolin' around with —"

"Oh what kind of baloney is that?"

"I'm serious. It's not baloney. Last night he was followed here but he didn't come home."

"That doesn't make any sense. Whatta you mean he come home but he didn't come here? That's crazy."

"That's not crazy. That's what I'm trying to find out. That's what I'm asking you. Where would he have gone? If he didn't come here at one o'clock last night — this morning — where would he have gone? Frances, I'm not tryin' to trap anybody. I'm really tryin' to help you find Jimmy, honest to God I am. Please don't get all uptight. I'm not trying to —"

"I don't know," she said, chewing on her thumbnail and pacing in and out of the kitchen. "I don't know."

"You don't know where he went last night, or you don't know whether to trust me anymore?"

"I don't know!" she cried out.

"Look, Frances, you can believe me or not, but just remember something. I didn't let you fall when you were a little kid and so help me, on my father's grave, I ain't gonna let you fall now. I don't know how else to put it."

She put her fists to her cheeks and looked as though she was going to scream. She stood in the middle of the room, beating slowly and evenly on her cheeks, tiny blows of indecision and frustration.

"Where would he go here? In the patch? He only goes three places here. He goes here — I mean — oh you know what I mean. And he goes to Ripulsky's. And he goes to my father's. And that's all."

"He doesn't go anyplace else here? He doesn't have any friends here he would go to their house? Huh?"

She shook her head slowly. "Not for months. Nobody invites him anymore. They just come around and borrow his guns and stuff. But all those guys — they don't even ask him to go shootin' with them anymore."

"Not even somebody —"

"I told you! I just told you! He goes to Ripulsky's and to my father's house and to here — oh shit. You know what I mean."

"Okay. Why would he go to your father's house?"

"He wouldn't. Not to his house. Behind his house. He planted a garden in the lot next door. He rented the ground. Don't ask me why he didn't do it out back in our yard. I don't know. He had to be right there next to my father's garden. I don't know what the hell that was all about, honest to God I don't. But Jimmy got into a thing with my father over tomatoes. And he'd go down there every night and cover the plants when it was below a certain temperature. I don't know anything about it. But it really got to be a big thing. He was gonna have tomatoes before my father did."

"And that's the only other place he goes?"

"Honest. Honest to God. The only other place I know about."

"But that's only two houses down, right?"

She nodded slowly. "May as well be two miles. Or two years."

"Frances, I have to go someplace. You gonna be all right?"

"Huh? All right? How do I know? Right now I feel like I'm gonna have the worst period headache I ever had in my life and my period ain't due for another week. And I'll be goddamned if I say 'isn't' again tonight. I'll be goddamned, I swear."

Balzic left without further fuss, feeling an urgency he couldn't explain. When he got out to his car, the radio was crackling with voices and static, one voice belonging to Desk Sergeant Joe Royer – God, Balzic thought, has the second watch come on already? – who told him that a certain agent Russell from the state Bureau of Drug Enforcement had been frantically trying to reach him for almost an hour. As soon as Balzic ended that conversation, officer Russell called him and, even through the static, Balzic could hear the edge in Russell's voice.

"You don't sound happy, Russell," Balzic said. "What's the matter?"

"Mario, you and I been friends for a long time —"

"You can skip that part and go right to the beef. Our friendship won't suffer."

"Oh it may, Mario, it may."

"All right, if it's gonna be like that, Russellini, then put it on me."

"It is gonna be like that. And I am gonna lay it on you. My boss wanted to call you in. He wanted to talk to you in here. Officially. You with me?"

"So far I am. But I don't like the 'officially' part already. And I don't know your boss. Don't even know his name."

"That's 'cause he's new. His name's Rilkin. And the point is —"

"I knew you were coming to it."

"Oh I'm comin' to it all right. The point is, nobody knows what caused you to do what you did but everybody knows the result."

"Come on, Russell, get to it. What'd I do?"

"You went to the spaghetti house with no name —"

"I told you I was goin'. Me. I told you. Remember?"

"I know. And then you got out there and nobody knows for sure what you did inside, but we know what you did outside and Rilkin wants your ass, because, uh, because they scattered after you left and they're still scattered."

"So?"

"So they were supposed to make a big move soon. They were supposed to make a trip to someplace in Virginia just over the Maryland line and pick up a large amount of finest Colombian and now they're scattered and Rilkin says it's your fault."

"Oh come on. How long you been watchin' these guys? Since yesterday morning? They never scattered before? Huh? And you're gonna blame it on me? Bullshit."

"I'm not gonna blame anything on you, Mario. We're friends, remember? And I'm the one calling you now because I convinced Rilkin I could get a reasonable explanation from you for what happened this afternoon."

"Whatta you mean a reasonable explanation? That punk asshole got smart with me and I run the window up on his neck. If you know what went on out there what're you askin' for?"

"Mario, look, my ass is on the line here. I have to have something to say. I'm the one who told you where to go. You're the one who gave me your assurance you wouldn't go muckin' around in our investigation. Now you go out there, you try to strangle one of their pistoleros and then they all take off in different directions and we don't know where they went. I — Mario, I got to have a better answer than 'some punk asshole got smart with me.'"

"Well like it or don't, that's the best answer I got."

"Oh shit, Mario, what did you say inside?"

"Hey, Russellini, my friend, I suddenly don't care about your boss. My advice to you is to get a transfer to another office. I wouldn't work for a guy who made me as upset as he's makin' you."

There was a pause and then another voice came on. "Chief Balzer, this is Superintendent Rilkin."

"Aw, I should've known, Russell. The name's Balzic. B-a-l-z-i-c. And any commanding officer who makes an inferior officer make the kind of call you just put Russell through is a chicken-shit. Make a man call somebody up and stand there behind him like a —"

"Now you listen to me, Balzer."

"Balzic! BALZIC! You as deaf as you are chickenshit?"

"Balzer, you better give your soul to God because your ass belongs to me, you hear me?"

"On the best day of your life and on the worst day of mine, my ass would still belong to me, and this is startin' to bore me. I know you probably love it. But fuck off anyway."

"Why you little small-town, small-time clown. Do you have any idea how many people I know after twenty years in federal service?"

"Three?"

"Why you sarcastic sonofa —"

"Two? I give up. How many?"

"There's a Republican administration in this state, Balzer. You have mucked up a major narcotics investigation. Three months' work —"

"Jee-suss, that long, huh? Wow."

"And you spooked them."

"Hey, Rumplerilkin, if your guys can't maintain surveillance over a bunch of guys who move dope in rented trucks out of a crossroads where there's only four businesses then you and your people need to go back to the classroom and get the training films out."

"Balzer, I'm through warning you. You've made an enemy. And I'm a bad —"

"I know, I know. A bad man to make an enemy of. Rilkin, if all my enemies were as dumb as you are I wouldn't have a problem in the world. Oh, incidentally, we got something like eight thousand registered voters where I work. I think maybe seven hundred of 'em are Republicans. So tell me about the administration in Harrisburg. Hey, Rilkin, do the world a favor. Have a stroke."

Balzic put the speaker back on its hook and turned off the volume so no call could be heard.

Nice work, Balzic thought, sitting and staring out the windshield at nothing. You made a point, you told an asshole off, you satisfied yourself emotionally, you got your friend Russell in a jackpot with his boss. Three for your team, one against. And it's just fucking wonderful that you may not have to look at Superintendent Rilkin ever in life, but Russell is looking at him right now, knowing that he was the man who told you where to go and who asked you politely not to muck up his investigation and you went there for reasons you can't even explain to yourself right now, and your friend is sitting there looking for a new ass. "That's just fucking swell," Balzic said aloud to the steering wheel.

He turned up the volume on the radio and called Royer and told him to give the call letters for Russell's base monitor. When he got an answer he asked for Superintendent Rilkin without identifying himself.

He was put on hold.

"Rilkin here."

"This is Balzic."

"We have nothing to say to each other, Balzer."

"Yes, we do. I abused a friendship with Officer Russell. For that I apologize. To him and to you."

"You know where to put your apology."

"I *am* putting it where it belongs. Officer Russell is not to be held accountable for my actions. In no way can he be held accountable."

"You don't tell me who to hold accountable. You don't tell me anything. What was said before stands. You made an enemy. Russell made a blunder. And I'll make both instances right."

Then came static.

Balzic put the speaker back on its hook and got out of the car and looked up at the sky, overcast and gray, looking more like fall than late spring. There was a breeze freshening out of the southwest. The temperature was dropping and the leaves on the hardwoods were starting to turn bottom up. Balzic guessed that rain would be falling within the hour. Several conflicting thoughts crossed his mind, the most vivid being that a flash flood would swamp the office of the Bureau of Drug Enforcement and that everyone would escape but Superintendent Rilkin. Rilkin would be swept into a storm sewer and would be attacked by a pack of rabid, overweight Democrats, all in a frenzy created by long weeks on amphetamines they had gotten on forged prescriptions.

"Shit," Balzic said aloud. This isn't a straw you grab at to make yourself feel good. This is a vapor, and a very puny one.

He set off down the street toward the house of Frances Romanelli's father, Mike Fiori. He knew it was only two houses away, but he couldn't remember if it was on the same side of the street as Frances Romanelli's or not. He knew he knew but he kept seeing Rilkin being torn apart by fat Democrats talking very fast and reminding each other not to leave a bone unturned.

Balzic knocked on the door and waited. He had picked the house on the same side as the Romanellis'. He knew he'd picked the right one because he could hear a radio playing polkas. Mike Fiori loved polkas. He was famous for his love of polkas. He loved them so much when he was younger that he belonged to all the Slavic social clubs in Rocksburg just to dance to them and he was always raising hell with the Sons of Italy band for not playing enough of them, for never playing enough of them.

Balzic finally erased the thought of Superintendent Rilkin dying at the hands of chemically speeding Democrats by thinking of Mike Fiori forty years ago stamping his feet exuberantly to the rhythm of a tuba and snare drum and the melody of a trumpet, clarinet, and accordion.

The whiteness of Mike Fiori's hair startled Balzic and made him stammer when the old man opened the door. The old man opened the door only far enough to expose one eye to Balzic. A polka buzzed and bumped quietly in the background over the old man's shoulder.

"Who you?" came Fiori's deep voice, reedy with age and wheezy from all those years of breathing coal dust.

"Mario Balzic."

"Whata want?"

Balzic stammered even more. "I want to see you."

"You see. Now whata want?"

"Uh, Mr. Fiori, uh, d'you remember me?"

The old man opened the door enough to expose both eyes. He did not seem pleased or even curious about Balzic's presence. And Balzic, though at this moment he could not say how he expected he would be greeted after these many years, was not prepared for this.

"Uh, Mr. Fiori, my father was, uh, he used to come here a lot, you know? And, uh —"

"I know."

"Uh, and, I, uh, had some things I thought we could talk about and I thought you'd remember me —"

"Sell some-a-ting?"

"No, no, no, I'm not a salesman, I just wanted to talk —"

"Tomorrow, I go sleepa now."

Balzic looked at his watch. It was barely after eight. Or had his watch stopped? He held it up to his eyes and watched the second hand sweeping around the face.

"You, uh, you feeling all right, Mr. Fiori?"

"Yah. Tired. Come backa tomorrow. I talka you then. Goo-bye." And he shut the door.

Well, Balzic thought, rubbing the bridge of his nose, I don't know what I expected but it sure wasn't that. He started to turn away, but the polka he'd heard reduced to a buzz and rhythmic bumping when Fiori opened the door was again playing at the volume it was when Balzic first approached the door.

"Is this guy tryin' to dance me around?" Balzic said aloud. He knocked again. Again the music quieted, but there was no other noise, no footsteps coming toward the door, nothing.

Again Balzic knocked.

The radio stopped and the lights went out.

Balzic shrugged and guessed that the old man really was going to sleep as he'd said and had probably turned the radio volume up by accident. Still, there was something about the way the old man had looked at him.

Balzic walked quickly off the tiny, square, concrete porch, up the walk to the side of the road, and out of sight of the house. Then he ducked between the next house and Frances Romanelli's house and came around to the back of Mike Fiori's house. He edged up to the rear door and saw no lights and continued around the side of the house and saw at once light dimly playing on the grass and evergreen shrubs at the side. He walked up to the window and heard the polka music as loud as he'd first heard it. He edged nearer to the window and through faded and grimy yellow curtains he saw that the old man was not getting ready for bed. Balzic felt both stupid and angry at once and almost did something even more stupid. He caught himself just as he was about to rap on the window. He didn't know what to do; he only knew that the last thing he should do was go rapping on the old man's window and disturbing his peace because there, in his living room with one small light on and the music playing loudly, Mike Fiori was dancing a polka with an imaginary partner.

The old man was dancing with his back to Balzic and Balzic felt his anger and his stupidity slip away into shame as he was now fast feeling like a peeper. Worse. Peepers look at someone's present. Balzic was standing there gawking at an old man's memory of his passion, and Balzic ducked away from the window before the old man could turn around and catch him with his mouth hanging open with shame at having intruded on one of the old man's more private moments.

Balzic walked quietly away from the house and stood at the

side of the road thinking of what he should do. There was a great deal he wanted to ask the old man about his son-in-law. But, unless Mike Fiori had mellowed immeasurably in the years since last they'd talked, Balzic knew the old man had meant it when he'd said to come back tomorrow. He wasn't called a rock for nothing. No one intimidated this old man. No one had done it in the years of union organizing and there was every probability that no one would do it now. A man's character might be slower to reveal itself as he aged, but it would not be much different at eighty than it had been in his forties and fifties. If the old man said to come back tomorrow, then he did not mean to sneak around the back and peek through the window.

As frustrating as the encounter with Mike Fiori had been, Balzic shrugged at last, because that's all he could do, and went back to his cruiser. He was suddenly famished. Not for food but for the company of his family. He could not remember the last time he had danced, but he felt that he should go home and at least hug his wife in circles around the kitchen.

Balzic came home to an empty house and a note on the coffee table near the TV. It said:

Mario, your mother is at the bingo at Hose Co. No. 1. Emily is sleeping over at Dorrie Brooks' house, and Marie is with me at the Mall movies. Green noodle and tuna salad in the fridge. Be home probably at 11:15. There's a Pirate game on TV if you're interested. All the rest is junk and reruns. Marie said the whole world is a rerun. Your mother got very upset with her. That's when I talked everybody into breaking out of this joint. Momma won't get stuck in the tunnel. Ha! We widened it last night. Been carrying the dirt out in my pantyhose. You remember what I look like? Are your eyes blue or brown?

Next time around I marry a pediatrician. I can count money when I don't have anybody to talk to.
S/The wife.

One of those nights, Balzic said to himself. Nerve warfare. Too many elbows. Not enough padding. People getting poked in their egos going through doorways. Make sure the stove is turned off and the windows are locked and everybody into the lifeboat . . . where did the day go? What did I eat? Where'd I eat lunch? I didn't eat lunch. Did I eat supper? I didn't eat supper. Who did I talk to today who loved me? I can't even remember if Ruth was up when I left this morning. A little while ago I was famished for my family. And now I'm just famished . . . green noodles and tuna in the fridge. God, I love green noodles and tuna and tomatoes and ripe olives and what else is in here, Balzic thought, taking the big ceramic bowl off the top shelf and putting it on the counter, closing the refrigerator door with his foot. Oh boy, vinegar and olive oil and garlic, that's right, a whole fucking clove chopped and scallions chopped and a little salt and pepper and there is no better cold food in this town tonight, oh my, get the wine, get the wine . . . if you can't hug your wife around the kitchen you can hug her food. . . .

Balzic sat at the kitchen table and sliced a piece of bread and poured a glass of Mondavi white table wine from a magnum and sighed and stood up and shucked his coat and tie and began to eat, slowly and carefully.

When he finished a mouthful of green noodles — what did Ruth call this? Tuna primavera? Huh? Why not? — when he finished a mouthful of that, then he bit some bread and chewed and swallowed that before he took a mouthful of the Mondavi white. What a wine. Jesus H. Christ. Absolutely no pretense, but get it on the tongue and let it do its stuff. When you die, Balzic, do you hear? Are you with me? When you die, please let it be with a dish full of straightforward food and a glass of no-nonsense wine. Simple, direct. And dee-licious!

Balzic's eyes were only partly open as he ate and drank. The

world was visual fuzz, but it couldn't have been clearer to his
nose or tongue.

He stopped eating when he was still a little hungry. He was
not often able to do that, but his pants were all feeling a little
snug in the last week or so and he had to do it. He put the dish
and fork and knife in the sink and poured another glass of the
Mondavi and took glass and bottle to the living room. He turned
to the channel that carried the Pirates' away games but left the
sound off. Baseball he loved, but the people who sat in front of
the microphones and pretended to reveal what was interesting
about the game gave him a general pain in the ass.

Baseball was skill and unlimited time — at least theoretically,
that is, if you didn't count travel schedules and cities that still
had stupid blue laws — and constant analysis and guesstimating
about what ought to be or what might have been, but above all
it was to any policeman's heart the epitome of instant justice.
Not a pitch was thrown that wasn't immediately judged. Nor a
swing, nor a struck ball, nor a runner attempting to advance a
base or to return to one, nor a fielder's catch or throw or indeed
his decision where to throw. Justice was swift and sure and,
except in rare cases, justice was irrevocable. And it was delivered by men dressed in blue — except in the goddamn American
League, Balzic groused to himself, where some clown thought it
was okay for umpires to wear a kind of mock-burgundy-colored
coat. Disgusting. As bad as these hideous uniforms the Pirates
had been wearing the past couple of years. Black shirts. Black
pants. Yellow shirts. Yellow pants. Yellow socks! God almighty,
baseball uniforms hadn't been the same since that jerk bought
that team out on the West Coast and told them to wear white
shoes and green shirts! Green! The only thing green that belonged on a baseball field was the goddamn grass. Grass! Not
green carpets. But grass!

And if you didn't turn the sound off on these guys with the
microphones, all you'd be hearing was some goddamn hype,
some helmet day, a T-shirt day, or bat day, or picture day, a
prize day, or fireworks day, or ball day, or poncho day, or ladies'
day, or kids' day, or senior citizens' day, or this town's day, or

that town's night. Hype, hype, hype. The bastards can never just tell you about the game. No. It's always pimp for this, shill for that, and if you're lucky they might tell you the score every half hour or so. They might even get the count right on the batter.

Balzic drank more wine and watched the game and fell asleep daydreaming in the recliner and never heard his family return. He was daydreaming of a day in 1971 when Mike Cuellar was pitching to Roberto Clemente and the left-handed Cuellar threw his best screwball low and away to the right-handed Clemente and expected to see a ground ball out to the second baseman because that should have been the result, only that was not *anybody* at the plate. That was Clemente and he hit that perfectly thrown screwball on a long hump-backed line over the centerfield wall and the look on Cuellar's face was unforgettable. Instant justice. Only sometimes it was a lot more complicated than it looked. Balzic felt so bad for Cuellar because Cuellar had done what he was supposed to do and it still went against him. He had put the pitch exactly where he knew it would do the most good and it didn't. Instant justice. Sometimes you were absolutely right and you were still wrong. Sometimes all you could say was that all your best effort did was get you screwed.

Balzic's daydream soon turned from Cuellar into a night dream into a silvery figure in some kind of storm and outstretched in the silvery figure's hand was a silvery cup with no bottom into which were tossed a shower of silvery coins that passed into and out of the silvery cup. The silvery figure seemed to trudge on though he was not moving much and the storm continued without letup and the coins continued to fall through the silvery cup with no bottom. . . .

Balzic awoke to the sound of a woman's voice asking about the state of the Equal Rights Amendment in western Pennsylvania. His eyes came open slowly and the images in front of him were not dreams. They came from the tube. He sat forward with a

start, catching sight of the time on the clock atop the TV set.
The sound from the TV was very loud.

Balzic glanced around and saw his mother on the couch, in
her chenille robe, her feet up, smiling none too lovingly at him.

"Don't ask why I not wake you up," she said. "I been tryin'
to wake you up, yo, since seven-thirty."

"Oh, Mom, Jesus Christ," Balzic said, putting his feet on the
floor and rubbing his eyes with his knuckles.

"Hey, kiddo, watcha you mouth. Ain't my fault you drink
alla the wine. You do that. Don't swear at me."

"Oh, Ma, Ma, how'd you let me sleep — how come nobody
else got me up?"

"Hey you. You looka that bottle right there. Rutha want
throw it out. I tell her, no, no. Let him see, boozy him, let hima
look just what he drink. My God, that'sa whole big bottle. You
have a party? Uh-huh. No, no. No party. Justa you. How's you
head — gonna blow up yet? Gonna go boom?"

Balzic licked his lips, scratched his head, and, putting all his
thoughts on it, stood up. He looked at the magnum bottle. It
was empty. And while his head was not quite ready for "boom"
it was very close to ready for "poof!" If he didn't get under a
hot shower soon, his sinuses were going to cause a swelling inside his skull that would be relieved only by pulling an eardrum
loose so his brains could go "poof!" out onto the floor.

"Where is everybody?" he asked.

"Hey, don'ta you know? Huh? Nice husband you. Nicea
daddy."

"Come on, Ma, cut it out. Where's everybody?"

"Oh you, that'sa nice. Cut it out. Huh. Nice talk, Sonny Boy.
Stay away all day yesterday. Drink alla wine lasta night. Can't
get up today. Don'ta know where nobody is. And then talka
smarty pantsa to me." She was smiling; she was bright; she was
cheerful; but there was an edge to her that sent him out of the
room without a reply.

And it was all very simple. He could become president, but
if he woke up with hangovers and didn't make it to work on
time, he was worse than a bum. Every self-respecting man who

cared about his family not only went to work every day but he also got there when he was supposed to. There was no showing up late because you were the boss. Every boss had a boss — everybody knew that. Everybody answered to somebody. And how could you answer if your tongue was thick with hangover?

Well, if you were lucky, you had a mother who would come and turn up the volume on the TV set to wake you when all else failed. And if you were doubly fortunate, your mother would make sure the empties were there for you to count. And if this was truly going to be your day, your mother would let you escape with only brush burns on your ego.

Balzic was going to give it one more try. As he was pulling off his clothes, he was going to ask once again where everybody was. He knew where his daughters were. He didn't know where his wife was. He was going to ask once more when he heard:

"Youa say something?"

"No, Ma. I didn't say anything."

"What?"

"Nothing, Ma. Nothing. I'm going to get cleaned up."

Balzic never even bothered to drive by City Hall. He called Desk Sergeant Vic Stramsky on his car radio and said that he was going to talk to a Mike Fiori and that if anybody from the second-floor meeting room wanted to know where he was, Stramsky was to lie.

"What kind of lie?"

"The simple ones are always the best," Balzic said and continued driving out to Mike Fiori's house. There were several things that had to be settled in Balzic's mind and, until they were, he was not going to be able to deal with Frances Romanelli, and nobody could settle those things as quickly or surely as her father. What's more, Balzic was confused and, as much as he didn't want to admit it, more than slightly hurt by the way the old man had acted last night. Added to that was a dull remorse for having not nurtured a friendship that had been so important to his father, and there was no question why Balzic was going where he was going.

At least there weren't any questions until he got to Mike Fiori's front door and got no response to his knocks. Standing there shifting his weight from foot to foot and looking around, Balzic was suddenly filled with questions, chief of which was why he was making a production out of a missing husband who was probably no more missing than Balzic was. Irresponsible, immature, sarcastic, idiotic probably, but missing? Not likely.

Face it, Balzic, he said to himself. There isn't anything you wouldn't run to in order to run away from those goddamn union negotiations.

After his third set of knocks, Balzic moved off the small front porch and started peeking in windows. By the time he got around to the back of the house, he saw as soon as he turned the corner why the old man hadn't answered the door: he was in his backyard garden, hoe in hand, chopping steadily and smoothly at the earth between rows of pepper plants.

The grape arbor was still there, weathered and tilting. But the plain pine table and benches that Balzic remembered were gone, replaced by a redwood table and metal chairs of unmatched shapes. He didn't have to close his eyes to re-create the scene: there were his father and Mike Fiori seated across from each other, the sleeves of their white shirts rolled up, their dark, baggy pants, in deference to the heat, pulled up over their knees, revealing white socks and ankle-high black shoes, and their yellowish white and sweat-stained straw hats pulled low over their eyes to block out the sun.

There were bees near the grape vines and in and out of the morning glories that grew nearby and words went forward and backward over their hum. On the table were the homemade red wine and bread and the pickled cherry peppers that set mouths and bellies on fire. . . .

"Hey. Hey! Whata you want?"

"What?"

"You. What'sa matter, you? Whata you want, huh?" The old man was leaning on the hoe handle and wiping his face with a large blue-and-white hanky. If his accent wasn't hard enough to understand, he doubled the problem by chewing leaf tobacco.

"I, uh, I came to talk to you."

"So?" The old man shrugged and spit and put his hanky in the back pocket of his bib overalls. Though the temperature was barely sixty degrees at this time of morning, he wore no shirt. "So? Wanna talk? Talk. Comea here."

Balzic moved toward the old man with what little confidence he had slipping away. He wasn't sure why these emotions he was having were so intense, but they were. And each step nearer the old man brought a newer, greater rise of emotion. When he got about five or six paces from the old man, he had to stop. Another step or two and if he didn't get control of himself, he would be sobbing. And then he knew. There was no great mystery about it. It wasn't the old man. It was how many times in his youth Balzic had been here in this backyard with his own father. And, more to the point, the emotion caught in his chest and throat was for all the times he had missed his father. . . .

"Well. What the hella you want? No. Ain't gonna talk? Yes? Gonna talk. Whicha you do?"

Balzic swallowed several times and cleared his throat. He looked directly at the old man and focused on him.

"I have to know, do you remember me?"

"First, you tella me who you are, then I tella you if I remember. Okay?"

"I'm Mario Balzic. I used to come here with my father. And you two used to sit over there under the grapes and eat peppers and drink wine and talk about the union."

"Oh. Uh-huh. Mario Balzic. Hmm. I was ata youa father's funeral. I know. You? You was a little boy. Then you wasa no come here no more. After die. You don'ta never come back. Now you comea back. Whata for? You shame?"

"Ashamed? No. Why should I be?"

"Why shoulda you be? Huh? Why you shoulda nota be? You youra father's son." The old man's face softened as though he might smile. He did not.

"I don't understand."

"That'sa right. You don't. That'sa why you no come back. You 'fraid gonna cry. Like before, when you comea toward me. You almosta cry. You shamea cry. That'sa why you never comea back. No hard to understand. That's okay. I forgivea you anyway. Good reason, bad reason. I forgivea you."

"I'm not sure I understand."

"Ahhh bullashit. You play dumba now. Don't be playa dumb here. I'ma too old. You no understand? You think. Pretty soon you understand."

Balzic looked at the ground and tried to collect his thoughts. It was not easy. This old man had always been an overpowering presence. Now, there was no question that Balzic was intimidated and if he did not soon lose this feeling he would be incapable of asking the old man anything.

"Mr. Fiori, uh, Mr. Fiori, I have to ask you some questions. I —"

"Why?" The old man's gaze was as direct as his question.

"Mr. Fiori, I'm the chief of police in Rocksburg. I told you that last night —"

"No. Lasta night alla you tella me was you not sell some-a-ting."

"Oh. Well, I am the chief of police —"

"You? Chiefa police? I be sonofabitch." The old man removed his sweat-soiled straw hat and scratched his head. He took out his hanky and wiped the inside of his hat and then wiped his entire head. "Hmm. Chiefa police. How you likea that?" He looked at his hat as he spoke, squinting up at Balzic before he put the hat back on and the hanky away. He spit and shook his head. "Somehow I think when you wasa little boy, you wasa not be chiefa police."

"What did you think I was going to be?"

The old man shook his head and spit. "I nota know. But nota chiefa police. No." The old man gazed at Balzic again, his eyes focusing in such a way as to make Balzic think this man could see in his heart, and he asked, "Youa good chiefa police? Huh? Everybody the same? No better for this one 'steada thata one? Huh?"

"I try," Balzic said. "It doesn't always work that way."

The old man laughed slowly. "Hey, that'sa you father talka now, huh? You father, he was alla time see three sides everything. He'sa go nutsa try to make everything comea out alla right. I tella him, hey, whena it geta down to the end, to the last, gotta make a pick. One, the other. No can alla day standin' around sayin' here and there, this and that, no, no. Gotta pick. Halfa wrong, halfa right — uh-uh. No, no. Halfa right gotta be alla right. Elsea, how cana you do? How cana hit in the head witha stick the boss, huh? No can do this. Stopa think? Huh? Finish, that'sa all. Boss hita you. Finish." The old man laughed again slowly and spit again.

"You hita ina head, huh, people?"

"I have. Yes."

"Witha stick?"

"Yes."

"Shoot?"

"Never. Not yet."

"Cana shoot?"

"I don't know. It would depend."

"Hm. Dependa, huh." The old man laughed slowly again. "Ona what?"

Balzic thought a moment, and he felt himself not measuring up to this test he was being given. "It would depend on a lot of things, Mr. Fiori. I just can't say right now."

"Can'ta say, huh? I cana say. I thinka for chiefa police, you makea you life very hard. I thinka better for you you be a little bita stupid, no?"

Balzic tried not to smile, but couldn't stop himself. "It would help sometimes to be a little dumber, yeah."

The old man looked up at the sky and then back at Balzic. "Well, whata you want? You wanta know 'bouta peppers? Huh? Garlic? Lettuce? Huh? Tomatoes, huh?"

"No, Mr. Fiori. I want to know about your son-in-law."

"He'sa no more son-in-law. He'sa expert ona tomatoes."

"Would you say that again, please? I didn't understand —"

"He'sa expert ona tomatoes. He'sa no more son-in-law. He'sa know everything. He'sa bullashit."

"Uh, Mr. Fiori, it's obvious you're not getting along too well with your son-in-law, but the fact is, he's missing and that's got your daughter a little scared. So if you can help me I'd —"

"Helpa you? Whata for? To finda him? No, no. He'sa better where he is. Ifa he'sa lost, shoulda stay lost."

"But your daughter's very upset, Mr. Fiori."

"He'sa know everything 'bouta tomatoes. He'sa plant firsta time this year. Never planta tomatoes before. Firsta timea thisa year. Now he'sa know everything. And you, you no seea my daughter sincea she was little girl. You know everything 'bouta her too?"

"No, sir, I didn't say that. I —"

"Whata say? Tella me again."

"I said she was very upset because her husband has not been at home too much in the last couple of days. He was gone for more than twenty-four hours at one stretch. He came home for a little while and then he took off again."

"He'sa crazy."

"Uh-huh. I see. Well, do you know where he might be going while he's been crazy?"

"Hey, Chiefa Police. I hoe my plants. I cuta my grass. I takea carea myself. I geta up early, I go to bed early. I don'ta watch where crazy Jimmy goes. Or when he goes. I'ma nota cop. You maybe, nota me. . . . You likea tomatoes, huh?"

Balzic nodded. "I like tomatoes. Sure."

"Maybe you comea back three, foura week. You geta nice tomatoes, huh?"

"Mr. Fiori, I have to, uh, I have to know when was the last time you saw your son-in-law."

"Hmm. Tomatoes, you know, you can'ta justa stick ina ground and make grow. No. Takesa lota time, lota work, lota think. Hard think, too. Not easy. Then it takes gooda dirt, gooda manure, gooda water, not too much, gooda food, and gooda air. Gotta have alla them. Anda moon. Moon very importa. You know —"

"Mr. Fiori, when did you see Jimmy Romanelli the last time?"

"I tolda you, I'ma nota cop. I don'ta watch for him. I watcha for my plants, makea grow. I don'ta watch nothin' else."

"Mr. Fiori, your son-in-law's in trouble —"

"You tella me, huh?"

"I'm not trying to tell you what you already know. I'm trying to tell you what you don't know."

"Aha. Okay. Go ahead. You try."

"I won't be — aw shit, Mr. Fiori, will you just listen?"

"Hey. You fathera teacha you talk likea that? To olda man, huh?"

"No sir."

"Then don'ta talk likea that. Anybody gonna swear here, gonna be me."

"Yes sir. But I have to know the answers to some of these questions —"

"Why?"

"Mr. Fiori, your daughter's been calling me, she's been calling everybody lookin' for her husband. She's almost hysterical at times. But the one she calls the most is me. And I'd like to help her out."

"Why?"

"Mr. Fiori, uh, Mr. Fiori, because it's my job."

"You job makea wife happy whena husband no come home? You musta be busy asa hell."

"Uh, Mr. Fiori, there's something else. Your son-in-law, uh, he's maybe got himself in some other trouble."

"Nota him. You be ina trouble, you gota get offa you ass. You gota go find. You stay home, no trouble. So how's he finda trouble? He'sa no go nowhere."

"Oh yes he does. He goes lots of places. And other police are watching him."

"Oh yeah? Whata they watcha for, huh? They watcha him fall asleep? They watcha him geta no-work checks, huh? They watcha him not geta food stamps? They watcha him makea his wife go? What the hella they watch?"

"They watch him associate with people who buy and sell drugs."

"You meana hang around with, no?"

"Yes."

"Drugs. What'sa this, drugs? What kind drugs?"

"Marijuana."

"Oh-oh. Hempa."

"You know about that?"

"I wasa in Africa, Northa Africa, before I comea America. Arabs smokea alla time. Me too. I wasa justa kid, workin' on a ship. I smokea." The old man shrugged.

"Lots of people smoke it, Mr. Fiori. But the fact is, it's a felony to have more —"

"Ah that's alla bullashit. Same likea Prohibish."

"Mr. Fiori, whether it's like Prohibition, whether the law's right or wrong, there are some people who make it their business to enforce it. And they don't fool around."

The old man spit and looked at the ground and chewed some more and spit again and then squinted up at Balzic.

"Hmm. You tella me, Chiefa Police? How manya times you think I hear thata same story in mya life, huh? Come on, come on, tella me. How manya times?"

It was Balzic's turn to look at the ground.

"What'sa matter, huh?" the old man said. "No cana guess? Huh. Lemme tella you. I'm a kid, I worka twelve hours a day. No lunch. No placea clean up. No nothin'. People tella boss, hey Mr. Boss, that'sa no good, he say, 'That'sa the law.' Anda people fight and geta kill and yearsa go by and then we worka ten hours day. And stilla little kidsa workin' and people comin' around and tellin' the boss, hey Mr. Boss, that'sa nota right, and he say, 'That'sa the law.'

"And more people fight and geta kill and then we only gotta work eight hours a day instead ten and people think maybe gotta pretty good, but we still workin' like hell, and John L. Lewis, he'sa tryina make better and peoplea fightin' and gettina kill and alla time it'sa boss say, 'That'sa the law. You breaka the law we gonna geta the cops and they gonna breaka you head.'

"And you know whata, Chiefa Police? That'sa what happen. Every goddamna time. The only thinga is, after so manya people geta kill, the law, it geta change. I meana, you cana talk anda talk anda talk untila you mouth hurt. Nothina happen. People get kill, worka stop, oh my God, here'sa come alla politish. Oh yeah. You puta blood on the ground, you gonna have politish makin' a speech, you cana bet. I'ma old man, and I'ma tellin' you, I never see not happena yet. Blood don't scare the boss. Oh no. He'sa used to blood. But it'sa scare the politish. It makea politish shit himself.

"And now I'ma gonna tella you something, Chiefa Police. I gonna give you lesson. Politish, he'sa never wanta see blood, 'causea that'sa vote. He's maybe takea money from boss, maybe for longa time, but here, America, boss he'sa only gota one vote. And politish, he'sa want his job. So maybe he'sa take money from the boss, but he'sa get votes from everybody. And, Chiefa Police, you listen, huh?"

"I'm listening," Balzic said.

"Good. 'Causea you supposed to know this. You spill enougha blood, you cana change any goddamna law 'cause politish wanna keep hisa job and no bossa cana buy alla votes. Nossir. And it don'ta makea no difference you talkin' about the coal mines or you talkin' abouta booze. You get enougha blood on the ground, peoplea geta scared, politish geta scared lose hisa job, and pretty soon, lawsa change."

"I don't doubt what you say for a minute, Mr. Fiori."

"Huh? You no doubt? Good."

"But until the law gets changed, a lot of people get hurt."

"That'sa what I'ma tell you."

"Well, see, that's the part I don't like. 'Cause that's when I got to go to work —"

"You don'ta breaka heads for no boss?"

"Come on, Mr. Fiori. I've served a few injunctions in my time, but I've never crashed any picket lines. Are you serious? You sat right over there with my father," Balzic said, pointing to the grape arbor, "and you ask me if I break heads for a company during a strike?"

"I know lotsa fathers, I know lotsa sons," the old man said, spitting out his old chew and putting in a fresh one.

"I'm sure you do. But I've never busted a workingman's head yet and unless one of 'em comes at me with a brick, I never will."

The old man grunted and worked the tobacco around in his cheek. "But now you tella me abouta this hempa law. And you tella me the copsa who check up ona you for that, they no fool around. Huh?"

"That's right, they don't."

"So what'sa difference, huh? You tella me."

Balzic shrugged. "I don't know, Mr. Fiori. Maybe enough people didn't get killed yet —"

"Aha, yeah, masure," the old man said, sputtering with laughter. "And whata you do, huh?"

"That's what I'm trying to tell you, Mr. Fiori. I'd like to get to people before they run into cops that really take their jobs serious."

"They jobs or the laws?"

"Both. To some of 'em it's the same thing. They don't make any distinction between the two. The law is the job, and the job is the law."

"They'rea crazy."

"Maybe so. Some of 'em are, I won't argue. But some of 'em got your son-in-law in mind. And I would like to find him. Do you know where he is?"

The old man took his hoe again and began to chop downward steadily and smoothly. "He'sa crazy too."

"Well, I won't give you any argument there. But, uh, Mr. Fiori, do you know where he is? It'd really solve a lot of problems if I could get him alone and talk to him."

The old man stopped hoeing again. "Boyohboy, you surea you father'sa son. That'sa him. Yeah. He'sa alla time gonna talka to people, gonna make 'em straight. Yessir. That'sa him. Little bita talk, what can hurt, that'sa what he'sa alla time say. You know what? Huh?"

"What?"

"Sometimes, huh? Sometimes, talk'sa bullashit. Peoplea look at you, see you lipsa move, they evena make their face right, but they don'ta hear one goddamna word. Nothin'. They likea donkey. You stilla gotta hit 'em with a stick."

"Uh-huh. You're probably right, Mr. Fiori. But, uh, so you're not going to tell me where your son-in-law is, huh?"

"Tomatoes," the old man said. "I know where mya tomatoes are. I know where hisa tomatoes are. Minesa grow, hisa finish. That'sa alla I know."

"Okay," Balzic said, backing away from the old man. "Okay. I can live with this for a while. I'll see you, Mr. Fiori."

The old man never looked up. He waved with the handle of the hoe, a slight gesture, hardly an interruption of his work, but it was enough for Balzic. It said good-bye. It also said if you come again and ask the same kinds of questions you'll hear answers much like the ones you've already heard.

For three days and two nights, life was not kind to Balzic. His mother was reminding him at least once every time he saw her about the empty magnum. The negotiators on the second floor of City Hall were reminding him that he was either late or stubborn or indifferent or insolent or hostile or mute. His men were speaking to him only when he spoke to them because mostly he was stubborn, insolent, hostile, or mute. Vinnie the bartender and the other regulars at Muscotti's were responding to his grunts and snarls with grunts and snarls of their own or else they were ignoring him. His daughters seemed to have vanished though Ruth kept assuring him that they were fine and said to say hi. Ruth thought that maybe it was time to take the storm windows down or else maybe it was time for him to take her out to eat or maybe they should go to a motel with a swimming pool for the weekend and forget about everything.

Mary Frances Romanelli didn't know what to say to him even though she was calling the station at least once an hour and she was setting an alarm for herself so she could call every hour around the clock. She wasn't sure about anything except that her husband was still missing and that she hadn't seen him for more than a couple of hours in the last four days. About that she was very sure and she was getting more sure by the minute that something had happened to him. She didn't know what had happened to him but something had. She was as sure that something had happened to him as she was confused about what it was, and she was so confused generally about the crazy direction her life seemed to be taking that she had not gone out of her house for any reason for three days. Outside was just more confusion, and she had more than she could deal with inside the walls of her husband's house.

As for Mike Fiori, he wasn't talking to Balzic about anything but tomatoes. In three conversations in three days, Balzic had been steered away from every mention of Jimmy Romanelli and had been led on a short course in tomato culture. Balzic found himself listening to lectures on how one grew tomatoes that tasted like tomatoes and not those pieces of round red mud that thieves and perverts tried to sell honest people in the winter.

If it all hadn't been so frustrating or if it had been happening to someone else, it might have been funny. But it wasn't happening to someone else and it wasn't funny. Especially not when Balzic got a registered letter from Harrisburg, on stationery embossed with the seal of the commonwealth and signed by somebody Balzic had never heard of in the attorney general's office telling him that while this was ". . . not an official reprimand nor was it to be construed in that light, nevertheless it has been learned that you, Mario Balzic, chief of Rocksburg PD, have seriously compromised a major investigation by agents of the Bureau of Drug Enforcement by your disregard for orthodox procedures and your flagrant disrespect for the office and persons of Superintendent Warren Harding Rilkin, agent in charge, Southwestern District. . . ."

It was about 6 P.M. on the third day of this last three-day period of discomfort that Balzic tacked the letter to the cork bulletin board next to the shotgun case. He stepped back and looked at the letter, sneering at first, then smiling ruefully, and then finally smiling approval of himself and his good works. It wasn't often that a man got a reprimand that was not official and wasn't to be construed as such but was a we're-watching-your-ass-anyway letter and when he did he should be grateful that he had a bulletin board and also that he was still in charge of thumbtacks. After all, lots of people got letters like this one and couldn't pin them up anywhere; they had lost either their tacks or their ability to use them and when that happened there was only one place to put that kind of letter. In the middle of your back — after you'd drawn a bull's-eye on it. . . .

Balzic seemed to be losing his sense of time. He was not eating right, but more than not eating right he missed eating with his family. He missed the sense of the time of day spent eating with people he loved, and because he did, all time seemed wrong. All he seemed to be thinking about was avoiding the union negotiations on the one hand and, on the other, trying to ease Frances Romanelli's persistent and deepening anxiety. In the middle loomed the broad, bowlegged figure of Mike Fiori, seemingly as everpresent and forbidding as the union negotiations, who reminded Balzic in every thought about him how important the role of a union was. Balzic felt pulled by his official need to be separate from the union his men belonged to and tugged by his personal need to know that his men were treated fairly, and every time he thought about the police union he would think about Mike Fiori and then about his own father and their union struggles. Worse, each phone call from Frances Romanelli, each plea from her for his help threw him right back on his inability to make any sense with her father, to turn the old man away from talk of his garden and his tomatoes. Every time Balzic brought up Jimmy Romanelli's name the old man referred in some way, directly or not, to tomatoes, mostly to the fact that his tomatoes would be growing and producing for a long time but that Jimmy's tomatoes were finished.

"Fasta, sure," the old man would say. "Buta finish. Done. Fasta, fasta, that'sa alla he want. Beata me. So what? So what? He'sa beata me. Now look. Finish. No more fasta tomatoes. . . ."

The old man's demeanor when he spoke about Jimmy's "fast" tomatoes bothered Balzic because it was not the demeanor of a satisfied man. There had plainly been a competition about who could produce tomatoes first and Jimmy had won. Now that his plants had produced, they seemed not only to have quit producing but to have died as well. It seemed very important for the old man to take Balzic over to Jimmy's garden — which was in the rear of the lot of the house between their houses and not behind his own house where Balzic had expected it to be.

"Why'd he plant it here instead of behind his own house?"

"Ahhh bullashit. He'sa say he want it to be same kinda dirt alamost. I tella him it no makea no difference. Dirt isa dirt, isa sweeta, isa sour, don'ta makea no difference if it'sa here or over there. No. He's gotta bother old lady livea here this house ina middle — ah, he'sa no good. No goddamna good. . . ."

Either the second day or the third — Balzic couldn't remember — he could have sworn the old man had tears in his eyes when he pointed out for either the second or third time that Jimmy's tomato plants were turning yellow and wilting and collapsing.

Balzic couldn't say exactly when he'd got the idea to talk to the old woman whose backyard Jimmy Romanelli rented in order to have soil as nearly alike as possible to his father-in-law's. But when he knocked on the old woman's door he could see that Frances Romanelli was looking through curtains at him on his right and that Mike Fiori was looking through curtains on his left. He wondered why it had taken so long for him to think of talking to this woman.

She came to the door with the aid of an aluminum cane with a tripod at the bottom. Her hair was yellow-white and carelessly cropped short. Her teeth were gone and, in addition to glasses on her face, she wore a rectangular magnifying glass on a braided ribbon around her neck.

"Oh, it's you," she said after craning her neck up at him for fully ten seconds. "I was wondering when you'd get around to me."

"Uh, forgive me, ma'am, but what's your name?"

"Skobolo. Missus. Every time you went next door to the one side or the other I tried to get up to catch you but you was always inside. And then when you came out you was in your car fast, zup, and I couldn't never catch you. I broke my hips."

"Both of them?"

"No. Huh? No, my hips. I broke it last year. Fell right down getting up from the toilet. I can't walk fast enough to keep up with you. You wanna come in?"

"Yes, ma'am. Is it all right?"

"All right? Shees, it's the — you're the first guest I had in so long I can't remember. Come on, come on, the place is a mess. I don't clean no more. I just red up. But I don't clean. I quit after I got back from the hospital with my hips. Sit anywhere. All I got's cold tea, you want some?"

"Yes, ma'am. You tell me where it is and I'll get it."

"Oh no, oh no, you're a guest. I gotta do it. Busted hips or not. Oh no, you sit down. I can do it." She made her way slowly across the room and into the kitchen.

While she was gone, Balzic looked around. The woman was right, she didn't clean. There was a depth of dust on certain flat places in the room that made Balzic want to keep standing in the center. The house was laid out identically to the Romanellis' and to Mike Fiori's, but it belonged to this woman and this woman had long ago given up throwing things away. Balzic had no doubt that if something had looked too heavy to her, she had learned to walk around it. He had known more than one woman who had surrendered to age and forgone cleaning. They cleaned up and threw out as long as they could bend over safely. When they passed bending over safely, they also tended to pass caring whether anyone else cared. If you came into their homes you either liked what you saw or you were shown the door; life was only a little longer and no one needed to be scolded about dust.

"No, oh no, I don't clean no more. All I do is wash my dishes," Mrs. Skobolo said, padding slowly back from the kitchen with a large glass of cold tea. "I don't have no lemon to put in there. And all I got's saccharin. Ain't supposed to eat sugar. Hope you like it."

Balzic took the tea and tasted it with enough care to show it mattered. "It's fine, I like it. Thank you."

"Oh good. Oh good. You can sit down. Just push those books off to one side." The books she referred to were old magazines, one of which he noticed was dated 1955.

"These are pretty old books," he said.

"Yeah, I don't buy no more. I just keep looking at the same ones. Well. You gonna sit down or ain't you?"

"Oh sure. Sure." Balzic set his glass of tea on the floor, made himself a place on the couch, and sat down. He picked up his tea and looked up to see the woman beaming at him.

"It's really been a long time, shees. Boy it feels good. So? Go 'head. Ask me questions. I'll tell you everything."

"Everything?"

"Sure. You wanna know about these crazy dagos, huh?"

"You mean Mr. Fiori and Mr. Romanelli?"

"Yeah. Well, Mr. Fiori used to be not crazy but I guess he's crazy now and young Jimmy he was really a nice young fella until he got laid off and then he got real crazy."

"How do you mean crazy? How'd he get crazy?"

"Well, he never planted a plant, not an onion, not a cucumber before this year. He never bothered. Then this year they got in a big argument —"

"Mr. Fiori and Mr. Romanelli?"

"Right. And the young one ended up screaming and hollering that anybody could plant plants and grow 'em, that didn't take no brains or nothing. And did the old man get mad, phew-ee! Shees, they were like they was gonna kill one another arguing about that."

"When was that?"

"Oh, the snow was melted and just laying in patches. You could see the grass. End of March I guess."

"And then what?"

"Then? Oh. Then nothing for a while. And then another big argument over his wife. He hit her and the old man really got crazy over that. Boy, he looked like he could've killed him."

"But he didn't."

"Well, if you don't think maybe that's what happened, how come you keep coming around here and talking to him?"

"Wait a minute, Mrs. Skobolo. Let's get a couple of things straight first. Like first, all I got is a bunch of complaints from a wife that her husband is missing. Second, every time I try to talk to her father about his son-in-law, all he wants to talk about is tomatoes. The daughter is really upset, she's really convinced something bad has happened to her husband, but she's the only person so far with that idea. Nobody else has said anything like that."

"Well whatta you keep comin' around for like you do?"

Balzic smiled and shrugged. "That would be a really long answer."

"Boy, shees, if there's anything I got it's plenty of time."

"Yeah. Well. I could tell you, but, uh, it would only be part of the truth. Uh, Mrs. Skobolo, do you know something else?"

"No, what?"

"No, I don't mean d'you want to know something. I mean do you have other things you can tell me?"

"Oh. Oh! Like what?"

"Well, like how long ago do you remember those two having an argument about the young one hitting the other one's daughter? Was that last week?"

"Last week? Oh no. Oh no. That was a long time ago."

"A month?"

"No. Oh no. Long time ago. Right after they was arguing about who could plant plants."

"Mrs. Skobolo, this is important. Are you sure it was this year, this spring? Could it have been last year?"

"Huh? Oh no. No. I would've remembered that."

Balzic cleared his throat and thought how he should put his next questions. "Uh, Mrs. Skobolo, d'you know what the date is?"

"Oh, my. You got me there. See, I don't even put a calendar up anymore. I don't care, see. They're all pretty much the same to me."

"Uh-huh. Well, tell me this then. Who'd you vote for for president last time?"

"For president? Shees, I gotta think. Oh, that was, uh, that was, oh sure! That was Ike. Yeah. Old Ike." She smiled brightly.

"Uh, what kind of job you think he's doing? Ike, I mean."

"Oh, good job. Yeah, I like Ike. He's a good man. Yessir. He'll stop that stuff over in Korea."

"You think so?"

"Oh sure. He'll go over just like he says, you watch."

"You think he'll go over there and stop the war then, huh?"

"Oh yeah. Hey, you're not drinkin' your tea. Ain't it any good?"

"Oh it's fine, it really is. Listen, about these arguments your neighbors are having, d'you remember what their first argument was about? Was it about the garden, or was it about Jimmy hitting his wife? Do you remember? It's really important."

"Well see, they was both mixed up."

"What was mixed up?"

"Them arguing."

"They were mixed up, or the arguments were mixed up?"

"The arguing. Both of 'em were mixed up together."

"Uh-huh. Do you mean when the two men would argue, what they would argue about was both things, the garden and the daughter?"

"Yeah. Right."

"So whatever they started to argue about, the other thing would come into it, is that right?"

"Yeah, that's right."

"So whenever you say they were arguing about the garden back when there was still snow on the ground but you could see patches of grass, they were also arguing about Jimmy hitting his wife, is that right?"

"Oh yeah," she said, nodding slowly but emphatically.

"And there's no doubt in your mind about that?"

"Oh no, oh no."

"But this could've happened last year too, couldn't it?"

"Oh no. He didn't, the young one, Jimmy, he didn't plant nothin' until this year."

"Uh, Mrs. Skobolo, how can you be so sure about that?"

"Oh that's easy. 'Cause I know everybody around here has a garden. That's when I eat like a queen, when the gardens are going. Sure. I go around and ask everybody if they got any extra and they always give me some."

"You eat good then, huh?"

"Good! Boy, shees, I eat like a queen. Yessir. And I get a whole bunch of bushel baskets full of sand in the fruit cellar me and my mister dug and I put all the roots in them, boy. I eat good for a long time. There's nothin' like vegetables — specially if you ain't got no teeth like I have. I get a good bone and make up a big pot of soup, boy, that's good. Queen of England ain't got nothin' on me, nossir."

"Do you, uh, don't you eat so good the rest of the time?"

"Oh I eat enough to live. You'd be surprised how long you can keep roots in sand. Long time. Yessir. Oh I do okay. Anyway, listen, I know who has gardens and who don't. And Jimmy, he don't plant nothing, not an onion, nossir, not till this year."

Balzic nodded and drank the rest of his tea. He stood up and motioned toward the kitchen with the glass as though to say he would put it in the sink. He came back and extended his hand to the old woman. "I want to thank you very much for your tea and for your help. I mean, I really enjoyed the tea and you really helped me a lot."

"Oh, shees, that's okay. You're more than welcome." She shook his hand solemnly, looking up at him brightly. "You gonna arrest him?"

"Uh, beg pardon?"

"Are you gonna arrest him?"

"Mr. Fiori?"

"Yeah, who else?"

"Should I? You think I should, huh?"

"Heck yes. He killed him."

Balzic let the old woman's hand slide gently out of his own. "He did, huh? Uh, Mrs. Skobolo, how do you know that?"

"I seen him buryin' him, I told you that!"

"Um, no, ma'am, you didn't tell me that. But that's all right. Tell me now."

"Well he did too! He buried him right out there." She motioned shakily over his shoulder with her thumb. "I saw him."

"Uh-huh. Now this is important. I know you told me you saw him and I know you told me when, but tell me again, now. When did you see him?"

"In my dream! Plain as my hand." She held her hand up in front of her face.

Balzic sighed and tried not to show it. "When did you have your dream, Mrs. Skobolo? Please remember carefully, okay?"

"Oh I have so many dreams it's hard to remember. Like I always have the same one about the ceiling falling down on me. But that's 'cause my mister got pinned in the mine once for two days when the roof fell. But he got out okay, but I still have that one, oh, two, three times a week. Then the other one I always have is I'm walking somewhere all alone and I can see for, oh, miles and miles and way off there's a church with an Orthodox cross on top and there're people out front and they're crossing themselves the Catholic way, you know left shoulder first instead the right and I tell 'em they're doing it backwards or else they're in the wrong church, but they never hear me 'cause it's so far away, and no matter how fast I walk toward them I always stay the same way away, you know what I mean?"

"You bet the numbers on your dreams, Mrs. Skobolo?"

"Huh? Oh yeah, I used to. I don't anymore. I haven't bought a dream book in, oh boy, must be ten years now. And nobody'll come by the house anymore and pick up your number like they used to. Now they're as bad as doctors. Neither one of 'em comes to your house. You know, somebody oughta make 'em. I can't go noplace anymore with my hips. You gotta have something to look forward to."

"You're right there, Mrs. Skobolo. Listen, about the dream where you saw Mr. Fiori kill Jimmy Romanelli, was it really a clear dream? I mean, did you see their faces and everything?"

"Oh sure. Oh sure, yeah."

"And where'd it happen?"

"In my bed! I was asleep."

"No, no. Where'd he kill him in your dream? Where were they? Did you see that?"

"Oh. I know what you mean. Why sure, it was clear as daylight. Right out back."

"In your backyard?"

"Yup. Clear as daylight."

"Uh, how'd it happen?"

"Why he walked up behind him with a shovel and hit him in the neck."

"With the shovel?"

"Sure. Right in the neck."

"There was no struggle, no fight, no argument, he just walked up behind him and hit him with a shovel in the neck and it was as clear as daylight, is that it?"

"Yessir. Just like that."

"What happened then, in your dream I mean?"

"Oh. Oh. I woke up. Nothing happened. That's right. I woke up then."

"And that was the end of your dream. Hmm. Where were you when you woke up, do you remember?"

"In bed."

"You're sure you were in bed. Couldn't it be you fell asleep on the couch or in a chair?"

"Oh no. I never do that."

"Never? You never lay on the couch?"

"Oh sometimes I guess I do."

"In the last couple of nights did you lay on the couch?"

"I don't think so. Uh-uh."

Balzic nodded, pursing his lips. "Okay, if you say so. Just, uh, just one more thing. How d'you feel about this dream?"

"How do I feel about it?"

"Yeah. Does it scare you? Does it worry you? Make you mad, make you uncomfortable? Make you nervous?"

"No. No, it don't make me none of those."

"Does it make you anything? Do you feel bad for Jimmy? You feel bad for Mr. Fiori? Anything like that?"

"Oh, they always were nice to me. I don't know. No, I ain't scared or nervous or nothing like that. No, I don't feel nothing, uh-uh."

"Did Jimmy deserve it?"

"No. No, I don't think so."

"Did the old man have a right to do that?"

"Well, Jimmy, I don't know, Jimmy shouldn't've hit his wife like that."

"I see. Well, tell me. Do you remember anything else about your dream?"

"No. No. Just the old man's face, that's all."

"What about it?"

"Oh, he looked, sort of, like he was, uh, I don't know, sort of right."

"I see. Sort of right. Well. Mrs. Skobolo, I really can't thank you enough. You've been very helpful. I should've come to you sooner."

"Well you couldn't've done nothing sooner. The first day you came around nothin' happened yet — I don't think."

Balzic said good-bye to the old woman with his mind spilling four different ways at once. His stomach was rumbling. He could taste acid and for a moment he thought he was going to be sick.

He got to his cruiser and opened the door and stood by it for almost a minute breathing deeply in an effort to relax his stomach. He glanced at Mike Fiori's house but didn't see the old man anywhere. In Jimmy Romanelli's house, the face of Frances Romanelli pulled back from the curtains in the front room. Then her front door opened and she was coming toward him. She seemed to Balzic paler, her skin starkly white against the blackness of her hair that fell wildly about her face. She looked thin as dry sticks. She came toward him in a kind of skittish hop, like a sparrow in winter, windblown and hungry, her fingers to her lips, her courage going and her fears rising. She seemed to Balzic to be utterly without hope; worse, without guile or grit. When she began to speak it was as though she believed she had no right to do anything but plead.

Balzic slumped into the cruiser and tried to prepare himself for her.

"I don't know what that woman told you, but I think you ought to know that she's —"

"What? Not right upstairs?" Balzic said, tapping his forehead.

"Yes. She's —"

"Frances," Balzic interrupted her again, "believe me, nobody's right upstairs." He closed the door and started the engine. "We're all stuck up there inside our own skulls and everything gets twisted around in there and there's not one of us walking around who's all right upstairs. That old lady's no worse than any of the rest of us —"

"But she is!"

"— and you'll just have to take my word on that 'cause I can't stay and talk."

"But there's some stuff I have to ask you."

"And there's some stuff I have to ask you too, but not now. I got other problems now. But I'll be back. I don't want to, but I will."

"What does that mean? For sure you're coming back?"

"Yes. I just got to go think somewhere."

"About Jimmy?"

"Sure about Jimmy. About your father, about everything."

"When are you coming back?"

"I don't know, Frances," he called out as he drove away. Then Stramsky's voice came crackling over the radio.

"Hey, Vic, there's a couple things —"

"Mario, you better get in here."

"Just a minute. There's a couple things, listen up. There's a woman named Skobolo, I want you to call the Senior Citizens

Center and put her name on their sheet, uh, put her down for Meals on Wheels and for the visiting nurse program, you got that?"

"Mario, there's a guy here from —"

"Vic, did you get what I just told you? Huh? About the woman."

"Aw shit. Give me the name again and the address."

Balzic repeated the name, spelling it, and then the address.

"Okay," said Stramsky. "Now you wanna listen to me or not?"

"Go ahead. But first tell me is Russell there?"

"Yeah, he's here. You gonna listen to me?"

"Go ahead. I'm listenin'."

"There's a guy here from the state narcs who wants a piece of you so bad he's makin' bubbles when he talks. He's waving so many pieces of paper around that I don't know really what the hell he wants."

"What kind of paper?"

"Show cause orders, arrest warrant, search warrant —"

"What's his name? Rilkin?"

"Yeah, that's him."

"Oh throw him the hell out."

"Mario, he's got another guy, a state deputy attorney general —"

"A what?"

"Yeah. A state deputy AG. They been beating on the mayor's ear and Renaldo's too for I don't know how long. Renaldo's really hit it off with these two."

"You can't put 'em off?"

"Mario, they're saying some really ugly stuff about you. And Renaldo's suckin' up to these guys so bad it makes me wanna puke."

"Well what's their bitch, exactly?"

"Obstruction of justice, interference with police officers, malfeasance, nonfeasance — that's all I can remember."

"Forget about it."

"Forget — Mario, they're driving me nuts in here. I —"

"Is Russell there?"

"Who?"

"Russell. Russellini. Is he there?"

"I told you before."

"Tell him to go for a walk. Tell him I'll pick him up down by that barber shop across from the A&P."

"How am I gonna work that, Mario? They're all together in here."

"You'll think of something, Vic. Look at it this way. If you know I ain't coming in — and I'm not — then you'll figure something out. It's important, Vic. He's the only one who'll listen. Tell him it'll help him more than it'll help me."

"Mario, Christ, why do you put me in places like this?"

"Vic, it's no big deal, just tell Russell to take a walk. And tell the rest of 'em that I ain't coming, period, so they can get off your back."

"Mario!"

"Do it, Vic. Please just do it, okay? I'm in the worst shit I ever been in in my life. Please just do it, okay?"

"Okay, Mario. I don't know how but I'll do it."

"Thank you."

Balzic forced himself to concentrate on driving because he didn't want to think about what he was going to have to do. The acid coming up from his stomach was so bad that he stopped at a drug store and got the strongest nonprescription antacid he could buy and chewed three tablets before he paid for them. If I don't get an ulcer over this one, he thought, I'll never get an ulcer over nothing. . . .

Then he turned the corner by the A&P and saw Russellini and forgot about his stomach. Russellini trotted across the street and got in.

"Mario, what the fuck're you doing, huh? What're you tryin' to do to me?"

"Take it easy, Russell, take it easy."

"Take it easy my ass. That guy with Rilkin is a deputy attorney general of the commonwealth — that's the whole fuckin' state in case you forgot —"

"I know."

"— that's Deputy Attorney General Muth? Criminal Division? In charge of the Bureau of Drug Enforcement and so forth and so on. You listenin' to me? My fucking boss in other words!"

"Thanks for coming, Russell, no shit, I mean it. Thank you. 'Cause I really got a problem."

Russell could do nothing but stare at Balzic.

"No, no, hey, Russell, I don't give a shit about that deputy AG—"

"Well I do goddamnit!"

"I'm sure you do. With good reason. But, uh, look. Just listen with an open mind for a couple of minutes."

"Where the hell you takin' me?"

"You'll see. We'll be there in a couple of minutes. Now listen. Let me straighten this out about this DAG. What's he doin' here anyway? Rilkin sure didn't bring him. Or did he? Huh?"

"Nah, he was at a fund-raiser in Pittsburgh and Rilkin thought it would really shake you up if he brought him over, if he had the time and so on, so the DAG had the time, and he was a little juiced, so he thought what the hell, it'd be fun and all that shit, and his chauffeur drove him over. Only now the sauce is wearin' off and he's really starting to get pissed standing around waitin' for you. And when he gets pissed it's guys like me that catch it 'cause him and Rilkin are buddies from way back. So Rilkin ain't gonna catch nothing. But I am!"

"Okay, listen to me now, okay? I don't care how pissed he is. And I don't care how good buddies he is with Rilkin. The facts are these, and they're simple: I hassled one of your subjects. Your subjects scattered. You guys can't find 'em, but that ain't my fault. And if that's what this DAG and Rilkin wanna hassle me about, they're dumber than I think and I think they're pretty dumb because no magistrate around here is gonna do me with more than a recognizance bond. Now you tell me: Is this Muth, whatever his name is, is he gonna come back and lead the prosecution? Huh? Is he?"

"Doesn't seem likely," Russell said, lowering his voice considerably.

"Not just not likely. More like never happen. Period. Where's the publicity? Where's the ink? The publicity and the ink are worse than no good to him. They're not there. Who cares that I got a magistrate's hearing on dumb shit like not doing my job? Tell me, Russell. Name one person besides my mother who's gonna think that's a big thing."

"Hey," Russell said, shrugging heavily, "what can I tell you?"

"Russell, these grandstanders, they make a lot of smoke, but no photographers? No TV cameras? No microphones? Forget it. They take their smoke machines and go home. Which still leaves me with my problem."

Balzic pulled off the edge of the macadam in front of Mike Fiori's house. "And Russell, you can't believe the kind of problem I got."

"What're you talking about? What're we doing — where the hell are we?"

"We're gonna go dig up one of the guys you guys are lookin' for. And you'll never know how much I don't want to be doing it." Balzic felt his eyes filling up and he turned quickly away from Russell and got out of the car.

When he came around the back of the car he saw the old man waiting for him at the side of the house.

Balzic thought his knees were going to buckle. His breath started coming faster and faster; his fingers were getting cold and tingly; he felt like he was standing with one foot in a ditch; his chest was growing very tight across his breastbone and through his pectoral muscles; he felt his throat muscles constricting. He wanted, suddenly and desperately, a large glass of very cold wine. Russell was gawking at him. Worst of all, he felt Mike Fiori's unflinching, unblinking gaze.

Balzic managed with great effort to swallow and to start walking. He could do that only by looking at the ground. He knew that if he tried to walk normally with his head up he'd lose his balance. He didn't know what he was going to say; worse, he didn't know if, when he tried, he'd be able to say anything.

He heard someone speaking to him. It was Russell.

"You all right? You look like you're drunk. You're staggering, for crissake."

"I ain't drunk. I just wish I was looking at a nigger junked up on speed and sweet wine instead of who I'm looking at."

"Mario, you sure you don't wanna get back in the car and sit down for a while? Huh? I mean, no shit, you don't look right."

"I ain't right. I don't feel right. But I am right and I wish to God I wasn't."

"Mario, don't get mad, okay," Russell said, "but I think you're delirious. You're sick, man. I mean it."

"Whata you want?" came Mike Fiori's voice.

Balzic put his fist to his mouth and swallowed with great effort. He felt tears on his cheeks. He let out a long, slow breath and said, "Mr. Fiori, I need shovels."

"Whata for?"

"I want to dig in your son-in-law's garden," Balzic said, rubbing his forehead and avoiding the old man's gaze.

"You wanna dig 'em up, you geta your own shovels. I no help."

"Please, Mr. Fiori, please don't make this any tougher than it is, okay? You don't have to get the shovels, just tell me where they are and I'll get them myself, okay?"

"Mario, what the fuck's goin' on?" Russell said.

"Hey, sonny boy. No swear. I'ma only onea swear here."

"Mario, what's goin' on? Who is this guy? You flipped out or what?"

Balzic sighed and shook his head and fought back his tears. "Please, Mr. Fiori, please. Please tell me where the shovels are."

"Youa cop. Go find. I noa stop you."

"Oh God," Balzic said and brushed past the old man, leaving Russell to gape at both of them. "Come on, Russell. Will you come on!"

"Mario, for crissake," Russell said, hurrying to catch up, "it's a good thing I know you for a long fuckin' time, otherwise you'd be on your own from, like, five minutes ago." He grabbed Balzic by the arm and turned him halfway around. "Will you stop and tell me what's happening here? Huh? You got tears in your eyes and your voice is squeakin' and you're staggering when you walk and you're askin' some croaker for shovels. What the —"

"He's no croaker. He's not nothin' snotty. Let's get that straight right now. And you don't wanna help me dig just go on back to the car —"

"I'll help you. And I won't get snotty about the old man if you'll just give me a —"

"Go back to the car and request the state police CID out here with a photographer and then get the coroner and after you do that —"

"Mario, you're fuckin' unbelievable!"

"— and after you do that, you go two houses down and you identify yourself to a woman named Romanelli and you stay with her until I tell you otherwise, okay?"

"The state CID, huh? What for?" Russell screamed. "Go two houses down, huh? What for? Why?"

" 'Cause if you ain't gonna help me look for shovels or help me dig when I find 'em, then you gotta help me that much." Tears were streaming down Balzic's cheeks now and his voice was breaking.

"Mario, you're not, honest to Christ, I'm your friend, I swear to God I am, but, Mario, you ain't acting right —"

"Just do what I ask you, please? Please? Call the CID and then stay with Mrs. Romanelli, okay?"

"Romanelli? Our guy?"

"Yes, your guy! What the hell d'you think I brought you out here for?"

"Okay, Mario. Okay, just take it easy. I'll do it. I will." Russell turned and trotted away, nearly colliding with Mike Fiori as the old man walked toward Balzic.

Balzic took off his glasses and wiped his eyes on his shoulders.

"Mr. Fiori, where d'you keep your tools — in that shed back there, huh?"

"You so smart, you finda out."

"Okay, okay," Balzic said, setting off toward the tiny shed on the other end of the garden. When he reached it, he had to remove his glasses again and wipe his eyes on his sleeves to clear them enough to see. The door of the shed, which was little more than a tarpaper lean-to, was held shut by a wooden peg shoved through two metal loops, one affixed to the frame. It wasn't a lock; it hardly qualified as a latch, but Balzic in his hurry shoved the peg deeper into the loops so that now it was jammed.

He closed his eyes in a fury at his own carelessness. He twice tried to push the peg back out the way it should have gone, but it wouldn't budge.

Balzic started at the sound of the old man's voice.

"Whata you gonna do now?" the old man asked evenly.

"Is there a shovel in here?"

"I don'ta know. Maybe. Maybe no."

"Quit playing with me, Mr. Fiori, goddamnit. Is there —"

"Don'ta shout. And don'ta swear. I'ma only one who shoutsa here. And I'ma only one who swearsa here."

"You the only one who grows tomatoes too? Huh? You the only one who's allowed to grow tomatoes? And you the only one who's allowed to hit your daughter, huh?"

The old man stepped backward a half step. "Anybody cana grow tomatoes," he said slowly.

"Yeah? Yeah?" Balzic's voice was quaking. He felt himself shiver and his fingers were colder and were tingling worse than ever. "Been anybody else . . . it'd've been anybody else I'd've been here and I would've beat on your ear without lettin' up for a minute . . . but it's you and I've been walking around on tiptoes 'cause I'm scared as hell of you — is there a goddamn shovel in there or not? Aw fuck it!" Balzic whirled around and kicked sidewards from the hip at the door and smashed the peg, causing the door to bounce open.

There was no light inside and Balzic had to grope. He threw three tools out, all hoes, before he came to a long-handled shovel. He stepped out of the shed into the fast-fading light and made straight for Jimmy Romanelli's tomato patch where the wilted, withered plants were now fallen to the ground. He looked at the ground closely to see if he could tell where the earth had recently been disturbed.

It took no great power of observation nor any knowledge of gardening. There was a rectangle of earth where some dying tomatoes stood out from other dying tomatoes because in the rectangle there were no weeds. The old man had taken the trouble to replant the dying tomato plants but he'd forgotten to turn over the earth around the rest of them.

Balzic began digging, took two shovelsful, and then stopped to remove his suit coat and tie and lay them on the ground nearby. He resumed digging and stayed in the one corner of the rectangle, concentrating on an area about one foot square. The earth came apart easily. Barely two feet down, he struck a shoe.

He got on his knees and reached down with his hands and scooped away the earth until a shoe and ankle were revealed. Balzic got to his feet and started to walk back toward the old man, who had remained standing by the shed.

He had gone no more than five steps when a door burst open at the rear of Jimmy Romanelli's house and Mary Frances Romanelli came running out just a step ahead of Russell. She was shouting and sobbing and cursing first her father and then her husband and then Balzic.

"Daddy! Daddy, goddamn you, Daddy, what did you do? Jimmy you bastard . . . you bastard! . . . You sent somebody to watch me, huh, while you're out here, you bastard, digging up my husband! Who do you think you are, goddamn you!"

She was in front of Balzic before he could prepare himself and she hit him on the ear, a stinging open-handed blow as he turned away at the last second when he saw her arm moving.

"What the hell are you doing to me?" she cried out and slapped Balzic again before Russell caught up to her and pinned her arms behind her.

"Oh my God, where is he? Where?" She struggled mightily in Russell's grip but it was no use. He was twice her size and knew what he was doing. "Where is he? Goddamn you, tell me!"

"Right there," Balzic said and pointed at the hole he'd dug. "Look if you want to."

She lurched and swayed back and forth until Russell allowed

her to move forward. She looked down, and a great quiet came over her. She stared at the uncovered shoe and ankle for what seemed a minute and then she threw back her head and erupted in a ferocious scream.

"Yot got her, Russell? Huh?" Balzic asked after she'd quit.

"I got her."

"Make sure, man. And don't let her loose."

"Is that, uh, that her husband?"

Balzic nodded.

"And the old guy, uh, is that her father?"

Balzic nodded again.

Russell moaned softly and shook his head.

Frances Romanelli caught her breath again and let out another mighty scream.

People from other houses in the patch were starting to come around. Balzic looked at some of them and said as clearly and as loudly as he could, "This is the police. Don't ask any questions, don't get in the way, just stay where you are. Better yet, go home."

The neighbors backed up but they didn't leave.

Frances Romanelli looked dangerously near being uncontrollable. She alternated between trying to wrestle away from Russell and throwing back her head to scream. Then she stopped in the middle of one of her screams and began to throw her head back rapidly in a series of blows at Russell's face. The first one caught him unaware and bloodied his mouth. He avoided the rest, but looked wearily and disgustedly at Balzic.

Balzic stepped in front of her and said, "Frances? D'you hear me? You got to settle down here or I'm gonna put handcuffs on you. Do you understand?"

"God," she sobbed. "Handcuffs. Sure. Why not? What difference would they make? . . . Where d'you think they put me? My husband, my father, my father, my husband . . . they just put me in jail for the rest of my life . . . the hell with your handcuffs and the hell with you too! All of you! All of you! . . . my father . . . God. . . ."

Balzic felt the old man beside him and he turned at the same time Russell called out a warning. The old man had raised his right hand and was about to strike his daughter. Balzic shoved the old man off balance and stepped in front of him.

"No more of that. Do you hear? No more."

"She'sa no talk to me likea that."

"Oh will you stop! You killed a man for doing it and now you're gonna do it?"

"I no killa for that."

"No? Then for what? 'Cause he grew tomatoes before you did?"

"He'sa no good. He'sa no work, he'sa bum. He'sa alla time know every-a-ting, but he'sa bum. He'sa littlea boy. Thingsa don't go hisa way, he'sa cry, cry, alla time cry. He'sa no man.

"And then he'sa hit her. Nota one time. Nota two times. Lotsa times, lots, lots . . ."

"And what did you do to me?" Frances cried out.

"You shuddupa you. Who you talka to — him? Thata bum? You talkina to me. I'ma you father. Don'ta forget!"

"Oh God, how could I before? How could I ever forget before? And now. Now! How am I supposed to forget now? You fixed it so I'll never forget!"

"Shuddupa you! He wasa no good. He wasa no take care you. He wasa hita you. He wasa tella me I'm old, stupida. Then he wasa make hide for money. For bad guys. Make likea big shot."

"Do you know what you did to me?" Frances said, sobbing. "Do you know what you're doing — what you did to me forever?"

"I know I stopa him. That's alla I know. If I no stopa him, who's stopa him, huh? Thisa cop? Or thisa one here? Thisa young Balzic? Him? Uh-uh. Nota him. He'sa like hisa father. See thisa side, thata side, talka this, talka that, thinka, thinka till his head hurt, thena what? Gotta come geta me anyway. And I go show him how to go hita the boss."

"That's enough, Mr. Fiori."

The old man laughed slowly. Meanly. "Oh-ho, you no wanna hear, huh? You likea her now, no wanna know what'sa what."

"It's not that, Mr. Fiori."

"Oh no? What then? Tella me. I wanta hear."

"You're talking about a friendship now."

"Friends?" The old man laughed again. "Is that whata you think? We wasa no friends, you jackass. I wasa teach. He wasa pupil. Teacha, pupila, they no cana be friends. He was a baby, likea this one." He pointed at the ground under the tomatoes.

"That's enough, Mr. Fiori."

"I no thinka so. I thinka time you grow up. You biga boy now."

"That's right, Mr. Fiori, I am," Balzic said, fighting back tears. "I am a big boy. And you're about to cross over a place you don't want to."

"No?"

"No. 'Cause you said all you're gonna say about my father for one day. 'Cause all of a sudden I ain't afraid of you anymore. 'Cause right now all you are to me is an old man who killed his son-in-law."

The old man laughed harder than before. "Oh no, oh no, young Balzic. Nota for you. I never be justa that for you. You would like, masure. Oh yeah. You hope I'ma just be that. But I no cana be justa that for you. And that'sa why you mad now. That'sa why you thinka you no 'fraid now. But youa know and Ia know, that'sa bullashit."

"What's he talking about?" Russell said.

"It's too complicated — d'you call the state CID? Huh?"

"Yeah. The coroner too. They'll be here."

"Complicated . . . complicated," Frances said, "oh God, how complicated. . . . Jimmy! Jimmeeeeeeeee . . . Daddy, Daddeeeeeeeee . . . Oh god you fixed me oh god you fixed me oh god you fixed me forever . . . forever . . . forever. . . ."

"Mario, I think we ought to get her to the hospital. She's really on the verge here."

"Go on, take her. I'll stay with him."

"I no run away," Mike Fiori said. "You all go to hell, I be here whena you come back."

"Mr. Fiori, why don't you keep quiet," Balzic said.

"Why don'ta you go to hell?"

"Russellini, get her out of here," Balzic said. "Go on. She's gonna really be in a bad way if she listens to any more of this."

Russell nodded and firmly steered Frances around the hole in the ground and away from the garden and out to Balzic's cruiser.

Balzic watched as Russell put her in the back and then went around to the driver's side, got in, and drove off. Then he turned back to Mike Fiori.

"You really put a job on her. There's no telling how much damage you did."

"You don'ta understand nothin'. You as dumb asa you father. If you no killa rabbits, they eata you whole goddamna garden. Alla you work goesa their belly. Everybody likea bunny rabbit, they cute, gota nice little pink nose, everybody'sa cry when you shoot, but you don't shoot you don't eat."

"Same-a-ting this one in the ground —"

"Not the same."

"Shuddupa you tilla I'ma finish."

Balzic glared at the old man and felt his esophagus burning, his heart pounding, his hands clenching and unclenching.

"Thisa one in the ground, he'sa okay, hunky-dory, when every-a-ting okay. Anybody cana be okay when every-a-ting's okay. But when you got to be okay is whena every-a-ting'sa not okay. When every-a-ting's alla go bad. Oh no. No. Not him. Him, he'sa good for makea shit, that's all. He eat, drink, makea shit. No work, no take carea wife.

"If I'ma no kill, he'sa rabbit, he'sa eat the whole goddamna garden, see?"

"Mr. Fiori, just to, uh, did you just happen to look at your daughter just now? Do you have any idea what you just did to her? Any idea at all?"

"She get over."

"Get over! Mr. Fiori, you're unbelievable! You're her father. And that is her husband and all you got to say is she'll get over it? When, do you think? In ten years? Or twenty?"

"Oh shuddupa you. You justa likea you old man. He'sa always see this, see that. Hunkies gota no guts. Alla time talking —"

"What did you say?"

"You hear. Hunkies gota no guts."

"Jesus Christ, to think of all the times I came here and watched my father practically worship you. And that's what you have to say about him?"

"It'sa truth!"

"Truth! Why you two-faced bastard!" Balzic stepped forward and caught the old man by the hair and shook him. "I've had enough of you. You sit down right here and you don't say another word until I tell you." Balzic shoved downward with both hands on top of Mike Fiori's head. Fiori's eyes popped wide. He went to his backside in a clumsy heap.

"Hunkies got no guts, huh?" Balzic said. "Well, I'm half hunky and half dago and you know what that makes me right now? Huh? That makes me all crazy right now! You better keep quiet 'cause if you're gonna talk you better hope the state police get here soon . . . Hunkies got no guts and you got no brains. Were you always this goddamn simpleminded? I can't believe it. I can't believe my father came here and, uh, and sat practically at your feet, goddamnit. To learn what?"

"To learn how bea man."

"Aw bullshit. No man does to his daughter what you did tonight."

"He'sa hit her! What'sa matter you. You no got children?"

"I got two daughters."

"Then whata hell'sa matter you no understand?"

"That's just the point. I do understand. You're the one who don't understand. You're standing here telling me about rabbits eating your garden and how you got to kill 'em or you'll starve, but your daughter's not a tomato plant or lettuce or anything else that belongs to you just 'cause you planted the seeds."

"You don'ta know nothin'," the old man said. "You biga fool asa you father."

"And shut up about my father goddamnit!"

"Ho boy, see? Don'ta see yet, huh?"

"Don't see what? What're you talkin' about?"

"Don'ta see how mada you get when I talka you father? Huh? You wanta killa me. And he'sa dead! I no cana hurt him witha talk. But how mada you get, huh? Then, dummy, how cana not see how mad I get whena bastard hits my little girl? Huh? How cana not see?"

"That's not the point," Balzic said.

"What'sa point, huh, you tella me, what'sa point?"

"The point is, you old bastard, I haven't killed you. Or doesn't that make any difference to you?"

"You killa me, you no killa me, no difference, you father alreadya dead. No changea nothing whata you do to me. I no do some-a-ting to this sonofabitch here" — the old man beat on the ground with the flat of his hand — "he'sa keep ona hita my girl. That'sa biga biga difference."

"That's some difference, all right," Balzic said. "She'll be going to head doctors for years trying to get out from under this mess — the mess you made right here."

"And how abouta you, huh? What'sa mess you father makea for you? Huh?"

"My father didn't make any messes for me."

"Oh-ho boy, that'sa good, that'sa good. No mess, huh? Every-a-time makea see this, see that, see top, see bottom, see backa side, fronta side, no mess, huh? You life's alla confuse."

Balzic blew out a long, heavy sigh. "Only when I run into people like you, Mr. Fiori. But I'll work it out. I don't know how just yet, and it may take me a long time, but I'll work it out. Either by myself or with somebody's help."

Balzic turned to see if the cars he heard pulling in front of the house were the state police. They were. And right behind the state police CID team came county Coroner Grimes. Behind him a few minutes later came Agent-in-Charge Rilkin and three of his men from the BDE. Balzic looked beyond them for a moment to see if somebody was trailing them who might pass for a deputy attorney general, but there was no one else.

Under other circumstances, Balzic would have walked over

to Rilkin and given him some steam, but these were not other circumstances. Balzic was too distracted by everything he'd been hearing from Fiori about his father and their association to give more than a second's thought to Rilkin.

Instead, Balzic talked with Lieutenant Walker Johnson, officer in charge of the CID, telling what he knew of the murder.

"Love these domestic disturbances," Johnson said after hearing from Balzic the barest summary of what had happened.

"There's a couple things bothering me, Mario, like his rights for one. D'you tell him what they were? Or do you remember?"

"I really don't know whether I did or not. You probably ought to take care of it."

"Well, Mario, it's not a question of me taking care of it. I mean, it's a question the DA's people are gonna want to have answered. Did you or didn't you — hell, you know what I mean."

"If you mean did I tell him what his rights were before I started digging," Balzic said, "I'll tell you right now that I don't know. But I'll also tell a magistrate and a judge and a jury that I did."

"Easy, my friend," Johnson said, laying his hand on Balzic's shoulder. "You a little testy about this one, aren't you?"

"Just a little."

"Well, come down a few degrees and try to remember that it's a friend talking to you now, okay?"

"Okay, okay, sorry. What else you want to know?"

"Did you, uh, did you by some stroke of luck or foresight happen to bring along a warrant before you started diggin' in this man's garden?"

"No. 'Cause it's not his garden. It's the deceased's garden. He rented the land from the lady who lives right there," Balzic said, pointing toward the house directly behind them. "The old man's house is over there and the deceased's house is over there." Balzic pointed to both houses as he spoke. "In other words, there's no way I lose this one on illegal search. And I wasn't on any fishing trip. I didn't dig up the whole goddamn yard. I went right to it. And you make sure your camera guy gets pictures of the ground without the weeds and the ground with the weeds and make sure somebody takes good measurements."

Johnson nodded. "We'll do that, we'll do that. Now just to get it clear in my mind, how did you know to go here, where you went? To start digging, I mean."

"The old lady in this house, Mrs. Skobolo, saw it happen. Only she didn't see it 'cause she thought she was dreaming. She's a little foggy, but she told me. If it hadn't been for her, I would've had to dig up everything."

"Okay, Mario, we'll be talking to her. I think that's about it."

"I'm glad it is, even though I know it isn't. But if I don't get some rest I'm gonna fall over."

"Where you gonna be if I need you?" Johnson said.

"Home. Talking to my mother. There's some stuff I got to talk to her about."

"Well then," Johnson said, "I won't bother you until tomorrow, how's that?"

"That's fine. Now if you'll just let me use one of your radios, I'll get a car out here and be on my way."

Balzic called for one of his own men to come and pick him up and when he got home he talked for a long time to his daughters, his wife, and his mother, in that order. What he learned was that his daughters were quarreling with each other, that his wife wasn't doing very well at mediating their quarrel, and that his mother really never understood what his father saw in Mike Fiori. All she knew was that he did as little as possible to make her comfortable and because of that she always mistrusted him.

"Didn't you ever talk about it with Pop?"

The old woman pursed her lips and closed her eyes and slowly shook her head no. "That was union business. I no talk with him about that. When I try, he says never mind. So? We no talk union business."

"God, Ma, you'll never know how much I wish you did. Didn't you even talk to him about what he thought of Fiori?"

"No. They work together to make things better, that's all he would say and that was enough for me. If I no like him, I stay away. And I stay away."

"Well do you think Pop respected him?"

"I don't know, not really."

Balzic was more than baffled by this. He was shaken by it. He wondered if he had imagined more to his father's relationship with Fiori than there ever could have been, and then he began to wonder why he would doubt himself. How was it possible to be so wrong — hell, he could ask questions like these forever of himself and still not find satisfaction. He focused again on his mother.

"Tell me something, Ma. Why d'you think he never got married again? Bringing up a girl like he did, that was, whew, I can't imagine trying to raise a kid by myself."

His mother shrugged. "I don't know. I don't think he like women too much."

Balzic felt his eyes widen. "You don't mean he was —"

"Oh no no no no no. I don't mean he'sa funny. No. I mean I think he don't like be around women. Some men like that. Not funny, you know — how they say now, huh? Gay? No. But don't likea women anyhow. He don't like me, for sure I know that. He never do nothing to make me feel nice, relax, you know, at home at his place, so I don't go.

"Hey, kiddo, all I know is you look tired. Big bags under your eyes. Go sleep, yo, forget about it for little while. It still be there tomorrow and day after and day after that, you see."

"I won't have to see. I know it'll be there."

And truly it was. Day after week after month.

Mike Fiori, after being arraigned and after spending two days and a night in the County Detention Center, was released on a property bond amounting to value equal to a current real estate appraisal of his house and lot. He returned home and continued to live more or less as he had lived before, working in his garden, tending to his house, taking long daily walks, cooking, and washing clothes. His attorney from the public defender's office got two continuances, the first of sixty days, the second of thirty, working on established practice that more time means forgetfulness and forgetfulness in the legal sense almost always means forgiveness.

Mrs. Skobolo died four days after the public defender got the second continuance. Her last sworn deposition contained repeated references to the meaning of death and gardens in regard to betting the numbers. Early in her deposition she thought death meant one; later she thought it meant zero. Tomatoes she was sure meant seven, but she didn't know why and she said that none of the combinations of one, zero, and seven had been lucky for her. The last thing she testified to in her deposition was that she thought her dream books were probably all out of date and that was why she hadn't hit a number in a long time.

Mary Frances Romanelli remained in Conemaugh General Hospital's mental health facility for ninety-five days, more or less. For the first ninety-one days she did not speak. When she began to speak, there flowed from her a river of extreme emotions about her father and her husband. She talked to anyone who would listen: orderlies, nurses, social workers, psychologists, psychiatrists, other patients, volunteers, visitors.

She presented theories on marriage and the family. She described endless details of birthday parties, graduation parties, New Year's Eve parties, and wedding anniversaries, both her parents' and her own, until listeners walked away from her in mid-sentence. She took up the story, anecdote, theory, or history with the next face she met from the point where she was when her previous listener departed. She regaled nurses with raunchy jokes, she prayed with custodians, she recounted her sexual encounters explicitly to everyone, and she told everything with the same expression, tone, and air of mighty and grave seriousness.

She explained how to starch clothes and how not to have satisfactory sex. She compared Maine to Idaho potatoes, red to black cherries, Boston to iceberg lettuce, fathers to husbands.

She explained why she had chewed her fingernails and how she had quit; she theorized that being bowlegged did not make a woman necessarily better suited to motherhood; she swore that, even though her husband and her father had both accused her at various times, she had never put sugar in the sauce she used on all her pasta; she proclaimed that cancer was not caused by anything you breathed but by not being able to laugh; she said that tomatoes grew by the moon as her father believed and that they flowered because the temperature reached a certain number — she forgot whether it was forty or fifty — as her husband believed.

Her most ardently told story was that if a shoe is planted it will not grow, and the moon or the temperature makes no difference. It also makes no difference if a foot is in it. It still will not grow, not even if watered, fertilized, and hoed regularly to let the soil get air and to kill the weeds. It will not grow, not even if a father — even one who was a devoted and experienced gardener — planted it.

She seemed to the staff to have talked nonstop for three days and four nights. She talked through barbiturates that would have felled a horse, one of the psychologists told Balzic when he came to ask how they had allowed her to slip away before dawn on the fourth night.

He came to ask because he thought there might be some explanation, no matter how feeble or fragile or farfetched, for why she had gone home to her father's house and hung herself in his kitchen while he slept. She had not used a chair; there was nothing in the ceiling to attach the heavy twine to. She had looped the twine over a cabinet door above the sink and had pushed all her weight against the other end of the twine around her neck until she was asphyxiated.

"For crissake," Balzic said, "you mean to tell me you don't know how she got out of here?"

The psychologist shrugged. "This is not a prison. We don't pride ourselves on our, uh, security — is that the word?"

"You know goddamn well what the word is. Have you read the coroner's report? Huh?"

The psychologist nodded. "I haven't given it a thorough read, but I've glanced at it — listen, I'm not so sure you're talking to the right —"

"The coroner's report said her stomach was empty. Nothing there. I've talked to some of the people who serve food here. They tell me she stopped eating a week ago. You didn't check that out?"

The psychologist coughed and frowned. "I think maybe you ought to be talking to somebody else —"

"I'll be glad to. Just tell me who was in charge when she got out."

"I, uh, I was. And before you ask, my name is Solinowitz, but because I was in charge doesn't mean that I was able —"

"Do you have any idea how hard it is to kill yourself that way? Huh? You ever see anybody do that? Huh?"

"No, but I really —"

"You know how much you gotta want to quit living to do that, huh? To put something around your neck and just push against it until you're dead? Huh? You know how long it takes? Three to four minutes. Think of it sometime, I mean, when you don't have anything else to do."

"That's really uncalled for."

"She didn't jump off a chair."

"And I have thought of it," Solinowitz said. "I think you're overlooking something."

"What's that?"

"The revenge factor. Did the woman not end her life in her father's house?"

Balzic nodded.

"And, uh, and didn't she use twine that he used in his garden? I mean, the coroner's report, as I read it, and again I say that I did not give it a thorough read, but the report made mention of the fact that the twine the woman used was prevalent in the house and much of it was found in the garden, uh, tying up tomato plants, holding them up to stakes, as I recall."

"What's your point?" Balzic said.

"My point is revenge, that's all. You're very upset with me.

You've decided that my negligence, I mean, the fact that she got away from here is what led directly to her suicide, and, uh, also, that she had quit eating should have been indicative to me — to all of us here — that something was gravely amiss, but what I'm trying to tell you is the revenge factor. The woman got away from us, to be sure, but she didn't jump off a bridge between here and her father's house. She didn't throw herself in front of a train. And both of those things could have been done. The possibilities were there. But she not only ran *from* us, is what I'm saying. She ran *to* him. You see what I'm getting at?"

"Some fucking consolation that is."

"It's no consolation at all. None. I just want you to be aware of it before you continue to berate me for my, uh, my lack of security here, that's all."

Balzic sighed and chewed his teeth. . . .

It was shortly thereafter that Michael Fiori's last great silence began. After talking with a priest about his daughter's soul and with the funeral director from Donelli's Funeral Home about her burial, he became absolutely and finally quiet.

He began, at the public defender's urging and with Balzic's vehement concurrence, a thirty-day examination in the same mental health clinic where his daughter had spent ninety-four of her last ninety-five days to determine his fitness to stand trial and to aid in his own defense.

With twenty days remaining in the examination period, Chief Clinical Psychologist Harry Moskowitz said in a memo to all officers of the court, that is, to the president judge of Conemaugh County Court of Common Pleas, the district attorney, and the public defender, that ". . . Michael Fiori is, in the opinion of the undersigned, incompetent to stand trial and incapable of aiding in his own defense for the very simple reason that he refuses to communicate either by word, expression, or gesture what his thoughts may be. He is not in the strictest sense catatonic because he is both ambulatory and independently and controllably hygienic. He simply refuses to acknowledge the communication of others. Given his advanced age and his present indisposition to respond in any manner to the social advances of others, it is my opinion that nothing would be accomplished by prosecuting this man in a court of law. . . ."

A Conemaugh County court en banc listened to that report and to the report of the pretrial investigation of a probation officer and then decided in favor of the public defender's motion to quash the indictment, on the ground that ". . . no public good would be accomplished, neither would justice be served . . ." by the prosecution of Michael Fiori.

Fiori's face showed not a flicker of understanding when he heard the decision of the court. He did not even nod to the county deputy sheriff who led him out of the courtroom and told him he was free to go. He walked the four miles from the courthouse to his home in Kennedy Township.

So far as anyone — including Balzic — knows, the old man spoke not a word about either the murder of his son-in-law or the suicide of his daughter; for that matter, the old man apparently spoke only as much as was necessary to carry on the daily business of living until his death a year to the week after his daughter had reported her husband missing.

Old man Fiori was found in his garden by the wife of the young couple who had moved into Mrs. Skobolo's house. The young woman had washed throw rugs and was hanging them in her backyard when she saw the old man slumped in his garden and called the police and the mutual aid ambulance service.

Patrolman Harry Lynch, long since removed from his job as a desk man, responded to the call, and, when he'd seen to it that Fiori's body had been delivered to the county coroner, he reported the old man's death to Balzic in Muscotti's. Balzic had had one of those bureaucratic days that left him feeling like he'd been attacked by a mob throwing damp sponges and so he was drinking draft beer and staring at the glass and trying hard to think about nothing. The news of Fiori's death registered in Balzic's diaphragm rather than in his brain and made each breath come with a wheezy edge on it.

"It was the damnedest thing," Lynch said. "There was this old man lyin' in there with all these tomato plants and they were just covered with the reddest, ripest tomatoes you ever saw.

And it ain't even the second week of June. I never knew you could grow tomatoes that fast, did you? I mean outside of a hothouse. D'you know you could grow 'em that fast around here?"

"Well, it's pretty obvious you can if you want to," Balzic said, feeling an old depression coming too near. "It never occurred to me until just now that that old bastard wanted to."

"Huh? You just lost me."

"They're all dead now anyway," Balzic said, conscious of his breathing getting shorter. "So it doesn't make any damn difference what I thought it was about. But I never thought it was about that, I really didn't. That's how much I know. . . ."

"Mario, I don't know what the hell you're talking about."

"Hey, Harry, forget about it, okay? You wanted to tell me something, you told me. So go back to work."

Lynch's head recoiled ever so slightly and he shot a questioning glance at Vinnie, who shrugged a don't-look-at-me shrug. Lynch sniffed once or twice and left, chewing the inside of his upper lip.

Vinnie approached Balzic and motioned to the glass. "Whatta you snappin' at him for? He only did what he thought was right. He thought you'd wanna know."

"Hey, paisan. Those guys, you remember what happened last year around this time, huh? When they went out on strike for ten days? You remember when I turned into the whole goddamn department?"

"I remember," Vinnie said, taking Balzic's glass and refilling it.

"You remember what they settled for? Never mind. I'll tell you. They got eight percent the first year, eight percent the second, and seven percent the third. They got a fifteen-percent increase in their uniform allowance. They got time and a half for all court time, no matter whether they're over forty hours or not. They got one of their own on the pension board. In other words, last year when they went out, I said they were right, 'cause they were. And when they got almost everything they wanted, I was happier than they were." Balzic sipped his beer and tried to make his breathing slower.

"But in the meantime, they don't earn it standin' around in here jawin' with me, and before you say anything smart, who I am is the chief, that's who."

"Hey, I ain't saying a word," Vinnie said. "Not a word."

"So when Harry comes in here and tells me that old man died in the middle of a patch of ripe tomatoes, I mean what am I supposed to do, huh? He turns my goddamn head inside out with that little piece of information and he doesn't even know it. But then what? Huh? Go back to work, that's what. Go back to work and forget about it."

"Hey, you convinced me," Vinnie said.

"You is not who I'm tryin' to convince," Balzic said, draining his glass and standing.

"No more?" Vinnie said.

Balzic shook his head and started for the door. He had to get out of there. That depression he'd felt earlier was nearer now, almost on him, and he knew that if he didn't get out of Muscotti's right then he was going to try to drink his way out of it.

He turned back at the door and said to Vinnie, "I don't get any consolation out of this, but at least this is where it started. . . ."

"I understand," Vinnie said, nodding.

Balzic left then, knowing that Vinnie did. But that wasn't any consolation either. And he was outside for fully five minutes, standing in the afternoon sun, before he got control of his breathing. He started walking toward the station thinking that he had to get back to work himself and that the really strange thing about breathing was that the only time you had it under control was when you didn't have to control it. He was almost to the station before an image of a garden, lush with heavy, ripe tomatoes crowded out his thoughts about breathing and then he knew how much he had to get back to work. He thought of a memo he needed to write to Mayor Angelo Bellotti concerning the latest bids on four-wheel-drive vehicles and he thought that would be a good way to unload some pressure. He stopped in mid-thought, his gaze attracted by movement across Main Street as a heavyset, fortyish man in a polyester gray suit got out of a four-door Ford that had the look of a company car. Balzic watched as the man patted some pockets, switched his briefcase from one hand to the other, glanced around, and started to walk away from the car.

Balzic looked both ways, waited for a break in traffic, and trotted across the street, thinking warmly, Now this is the sort of police work I can get into. Nice, simple parking violation in progress.

"Hey," he called out. "Ho! You! With the briefcase. You gonna put some money in the meter or what?"

K.C. CONSTANTINE

lives in Pennsylvania and belongs to the world Mario Balzic works in. To date, there are five volumes in the Balzic series: *The Rocksburg Railroad Murders*, *The Man Who Liked to Look at Himself*, *The Blank Page*, *A Fix Like This*, and *The Man Who Liked Slow Tomatoes*. Two of them, with an Afterword by Robin W. Winks — *The Rocksburg Railroad Murders* and *The Blank Page* — are reprinted in trade paperback as the first *Godine Double Detective*.

THE MAN WHO LIKED SLOW TOMATOES

has been set in Linotype Janson, an old style face first issued by Anton Janson in Leipsic between 1660 and 1687, and typical of the Low Country designs broadly disseminated throughout Europe and the British Isles during the seventeenth century. The contemporary versions of this eminently readable and widely employed typeface are based upon type cast from the original matrices, now in the possession of the Stempel Type Foundry in Frankfurt, Germany. The book has been set by American–Stratford Graphic Services, Inc., Brattleboro, Vermont, and printed and bound by The Alpine Press, Stoughton, Massachusetts.

Illustrations by
Jan Adkins